Omensford Series – Book 7

Gnomes & Necromancy

G Clatworthy

ISBN: 978-1-915516-29-9

Foreword

The Omensford witches first arrived in my writing in <u>Attack on Avalon</u> (book 5 in the Rise of the Dragons series), but they were too interesting to leave there so they had to have their own book. And so, this series was born, based around the fictional town of Omensford in the Cotswolds and the witches who live there.

A special thank you to my amazing typo hunters, grammar gurus, and plot pickers who got this story to where it is today. You are awesome!

If you want to support Gemma, you can find her on www.patreon.com/G_Clatworthy for exclusive first reads of new stories. You can also join her newsletter at www.gemmaclatworthy.com for a free short story based on one of the witches in the Omensford series and follow Gemma on www.instagram.com/gemmaclatworthy, www.facebook.com/gemmaclatworthy or join the readers' group on Facebook: Gemma's book wyrms.

Chapter 1

"Come on, Mr Kite. Please."

He stared at Fi with a vacant expression, his jaw slack. A car horn blared behind her. She whirled round. "Alright, I'm trying, aren't I?"

Do you want me to trip him up? Cressida, Fi's wyrm familiar, spoke in her mind.

"Let's keep that as option B."

Spreading her arms wide, Fi nodded to the young police officer helping her. He waved his arms from the other side and they finally herded the man off the main road. The car tooted its thanks with a double beep and Fi gave it a wave before turning back to the short man in front of her. Now safely off the road, he stared at a shop window, tilting his head back and forth as if studying his reflection through his filmy eyes.

Fi shook her head. Sometimes her job as a Magical Liaison Office community agent was less than glamourous. And a lot of the time, she suspected that the local police fobbed off any minor disturbance to her, whether or not magic was suspected.

Unfortunately, in this case, they were right. She sensed something magical around the man as soon as she'd got to the scene, something that felt cold and empty. She hadn't encountered that type of magic before, but the important thing was that whatever had happened to Mr Kite, it was magical, and that meant she had to deal with it.

"Alright, Mr Kite. I think we'd better get you to the hospital until whatever potion you took wears off. I don't suppose you remember what it was?" There was a hint of hope to her voice. If she knew what he'd taken, she might be able to look up a remedy on the Magical Liaison Office database.

Mr Kite groaned in response.

"Everything alright, Fi?"

Fi nodded distractedly at her sister. "Just getting Mr Kite here to hospital, aren't we Mr Kite? Hospital. Good." She raised her voice like he was a foreigner who couldn't speak English.

"What happened to him?"

"Not sure, he's got a faint magical aura round him. It feels weird, and I haven't encountered it before. My best guess is he took a potion, or maybe someone cast a spell on him…"

"We shouldn't discuss a case with civilians," the officer said, his eyes boggling at Fi's lack of protocol.

Fi gave him a smile. "She's not a civilian; she's my sister. And would you rather take the lead on this one? Because I've got plans this evening…"

He lowered his eyes and shook his head. She was the senior figure in magical cases and he could jog on if he didn't like it.

Agatha closed her eyes and Fi felt the sensation of thorns scraping against her skin as her sister reached out with her own magic. Fi rubbed her arm and watched Agatha's reaction as she shuddered and clutched her bouquet of bright flowers to her chest.

"Whatever it is, it doesn't like my magic. Will you be done in time for the party?"

"Yep. I'll have to pop back to Mum's to pick up your gift, but I'll be there. What are the flowers for?"

"Sita saw me and insisted I take them. Isn't she sweet? So thoughtful, and look, she's put in all my favourites; tea roses, ox eye daisies…"

"Lovely." Fi cut her sister off before she got an extensive list of all the blooms in the bouquet. "Do you need me to bring anything else?"

"Just the cake. You did make it, right?"

"Of course!"

"Great. Now I'd better find Neville; he wanted to do some last minute shopping."

"I saw him head into Luscious Laces." Fi's mouth turned down at the thought of her brother-in-law buying underwear for her sister. There were some things a mind shouldn't picture.

"Oh." Agatha blushed. "Maybe I'll just meet him back home. If you see him, would you let him know?"

"Sure."

"So what are we going to do?" the policeman asked.

"Not sure…"

You could use your magic. Cressida brushed up against Fi's legs as she made the suggestion. The dragon-like creature knew that Fi had a guilt / hate relationship with her power. On the one hand, her electrical power had saved lives, but at what cost? Fi still woke up in cold sweats to images of people, and toads, who had perished at her hands.

But Mr Kite was under some sort of enchantment. Maybe she could use a tiny bit of her electrical magic…it wasn't like she had any other ideas, and it might shock him out of the trance. She'd had luck with that in the past and she had better control of her power now, so she didn't think she'd kill him…but…

"Aunty Fi!" A small girl collided with Fi's legs, rocking her on the uneven cobblestone pavement.

"Bumble Bea!" She scruffed her niece's hair. "Your Mum's gone back home to prep for the big party."

"Fiona! Glad to see you. Do you think Agatha would like this?" Neville reached his hand into the Luscious Lace bag.

Fi blanched and held up her hands. "I don't think I'm the right person to ask."

"But you're her sister."

"Exactly," she muttered. In a louder voice, she said, "I'm sure she'll love whatever you've got her."

"Told you, Dad."

Fi shivered. What sort of man took his daughter underwear shopping for his wife?

"OK, well we'll leave you to it. See you later."

"Bye, Aunty Fi."

Fi waved them off and faced Mr Kite again. He was still obsessed with the shop window. She shook herself. Time to try her magic.

"Mr Kite, I'm going to give you a small electric shock. It might sting a little."

Fi approached the oblivious man and placed a hand on his cool skin, allowing the tiniest trickle of her electrical magic to flow into his body. He jerked reflexively but kept studying his reflection. That didn't work.

"OK, hospital it is. If you wouldn't mind, Officer Clark."

Fi grasped one of the man's arms, glad he wasn't sweaty in the sun. His skin was cool to the touch and Fi tried not to stare at his long fingernails. The officer grabbed the other and they marched him to the waiting squad car. Three paces later, Mr Kite slumped down between them, his eyes rolling back in his head.

"What the–?" Fi started, dropping to the ground beside him. She took his pulse. "He's…dead."

"What?" The young officer knelt next to her and mirrored her actions. When he couldn't find a pulse, he started CPR.

Fi stared at the deceased man. People didn't drop dead that suddenly, did they? In her experience, there was always a cause. She took a step back. That cause was usually her.

Fi shook her head as she called an ambulance and gave their location in a daze, unable to meet the dead man's staring eyes.

"What did you do?" panted the policeman between compressions.

"Nothing…"

"You used your magic."

"No, it wasn't…" Fi broke off. She had barely let any electricity through, but there he was on the floor. Dead.

Chapter 2

Fi gave her statement to Detective Ledd and asked for a copy for her own report. One thing the Magical Liaison Office loved was paperwork.

"So, you say you shocked him with your magic…" the detective repeated with a tone that managed to mix dogged fact-checking with incredulity.

"Yes, but it was barely anything. Definitely less than mains power."

"Can you be more specific?"

"Somewhere between mains and a nine-volt battery."

Really specific.

"What do you know about electrics?"

"I beg your pardon."

"Sorry, not you. I was talking to her." Fi gestured at her familiar, now curled around her neck. It was comforting to have Cressida close, but she was hot and sweat already leaked through Fi's t-shirt thanks to a combination of the warm weather and her nerves.

A burst of coffee filled her nostrils as the café door opened. Caffeine. That was what she needed.

"I don't suppose we could take this inside the coffee shop? I think I need something for the shock."

"Yes, I imagine it's quite alarming to see someone drop down in front of you after you used your powers."

"It wasn't like that. Ask Officer Clark, it wasn't instant. He walked to the edge of the pavement and then dropped down, like he just stopped. That's not how my magic works." Not the way she'd used it this time, anyway.

The detective scribbled in his notebook. Fi twisted her hair out of its ponytail and retied it. He couldn't really suspect that she had killed someone. They'd worked together on a number of cases now and caught criminals. He had to know that she wouldn't just kill someone. He'd seen her protect a sentient killer pumpkin for goddess' sake.

He tucked his notebook away and gestured to the café. Fi fell into step with him, grateful for the small truce.

"Look, Fiona, I believe you…"

"Yes, I knew–" she nodded.

He held up a chubby hand. "I believe you, but this doesn't look good. You use your power and someone's dead. People don't know how magic works, they'll jump to automatic conclusions."

People. He meant mundanes or those without magic. They made up the majority of the population and they wouldn't understand.

She smiled weakly as a couple held the door open for them and walked into the coffee shop. The rich aroma of roasted beans surrounded her. Fi closed her eyes and inhaled, the familiar scent grounding her. She ordered a black coffee and the detective asked for a tea from the werewolf behind the counter.

Detective Ledd sat at a table in the corner and Fi sank into a chair opposite him.

"So, what can we do?"

"First, we hope this doesn't get into the press, because they will have a field day."

"Got it."

"Second, we follow the evidence. The coroner will look at the body tomorrow. We'll know more then."

"I want to be there."

He shook his head. "Not a good idea. There's a conflict."

"Like dzrak there's a conflict." The detective winced at the Dwarfish curse word that fell from Fi's lips. "I didn't kill him. I need to investigate this. There was some sort of magic on him, I felt it. What if that killed him?"

"We've only got your word for that."

I felt it. Something...odd, like meat that's gone bad.

"Cressida felt it."

"The wyrm that only you can speak to?"

Her familiar hissed at the overweight detective.

"My sister felt it too…" Fi trailed off as the detective raised a bushy eyebrow, making it look like a caterpillar had wandered onto his forehead. A relative. That didn't look good.

"Look, we haven't got any evidence to keep you, so you're free to go. Just don't leave the area."

Fi stared at the detective. "I'm not leaving because I didn't do anything wrong."

"I know."

"And when you get some evidence," Fi spat the word, "I expect to be brought back into this investigation."

"Of course."

Fi clenched her fists in irritation while the detective leant back and eyed her. She crossed her arms. She was ninety-nine point nine per cent sure she hadn't killed that man with her magic. Fi swallowed. Maybe she wasn't as in control as she'd thought. But barely a trickle had escaped her fingers when she'd shocked him. She was eighty per cent sure she hadn't caused his death.

"One coffee, black and one tea with extra milk and tea bag in."

Fi grabbed for the coffee and clutched it like the lifeline it was.

"You going to Agatha's party later?" Steve asked as he placed the tea on the table, oblivious to the tension steaming between Fi and the detective.

"Yes, yes, I'm going. You?"

"Yep. Glen's picking me up in half an hour."

"Are you closing the shop?"

"Nope, Valentine's agreed to wake up early and close up." The werewolf checked the large clock hung on one of the walls. "Speaking of, I'd better go give him a knock. See you later."

"Going to a party?" The detective fiddled with his watch as he made small talk, the screen catching the light in the small café.

"My sister's birthday. What's that?"

"It's my new smartwatch, do you like it? I'm on a health kick, but the stupid thing keeps giving me alerts." He thrust it at her face and Fi blinked. The alert said that he'd sat still for too long. Now that he'd mentioned it, the detective wasn't quite so chubby as the last time she'd seen him; more podgy than pudgy.

She shrugged. "Maybe the settings are off, do you want me to take a look?"

Fi watched the indecision race across his face. On the one hand, he knew she was good with technology and electrical items, but on the other, she also broke them, and she was a potential murder suspect. Even though Fi was seventy per cent sure she hadn't killed someone. Again. Please, not again. She wasn't sure her soul could take the guilt that already had her waking in cold sweats in the middle of the night. Her lack of confidence in her magic made her irritable.

"Oh, give it here." She held out her hand, saving him from his internal conflict and tapped the watch, finding the settings and adjusting it. "There you go." She didn't tell him that she'd shortened the alert time. It was petty revenge for him thinking she was a killer, but it was all she had. After all, she was more than fifty per cent sure she hadn't killed anyone.

Her phone beeped and she stood. "Thanks for the coffee. I'm going to the party. Call me when you realise I'm innocent and can help."

Chapter 3

Fi shifted the large package under her arm as she opened the gate. She closed it behind her and aimed a foot at the oversized cockerel that eyed her laces, shooing him away. Fi knew better than to antagonise Cluck Norris, especially when she was in converse trainers – not the best protection against a vicious beak. But Cluck wasn't interested in terrorising her today, instead he turned his beady chicken eyes to a flower bed and scratched in the rich dirt, digging for worms.

Fi stepped around him and headed for the back garden. She adjusted her grip on the huge package, making it look heavier than it was. The low hum of people enjoying themselves grew louder as she approached.

"Fi! You made it!" Agatha said, pulling Fi into a hug.

"Of course, I did. I wouldn't miss my big sister's big birthday!"

"The case?"

"Don't worry about it. I can't do anything until we get the coroner's report."

Agatha raised her hands to her face. "He died?"

"Oh, yes." Fi stared at her feet, unsure how to get out of this conversation. She decided to change the subject. "Happy Birthday!"

"You didn't have to get me anything."

"Nonsense. I'm sure you'll love it."

Agatha stared hard at her sister and Fi had to fake a coughing fit to cover the smirk that tweaked the corners of her mouth. She had come on too strong about the present, Agatha would guess it was something awful.

"Let me take it." Agatha held out her hands.

"No, no, I'll put it with your other presents."

Agatha pursed her lips.

"I'd love a drink, though, if you've got any lager?" Fi breathed out a sigh as her sister nodded, Agatha's desire to help people overcoming her suspicion of her sister. Fi headed over to the picnic table laden with presents and almost tripped over her niece.

"Aunty Fi!"

"Bumble Bea! How's my favourite niece?"

"I'm your only niece."

"Must be my favourite then. Let me put this down then I'll come say hi properly."

"What is it?"

"It's a surprise, but I bet your mum will love it as much as I loved her present last year."

"The socks?"

"The socks."

Fi turned so her niece wouldn't see her grimace at the mention of the ugliest socks in the world. Where did you even find knee high socks with a scrawny chicken leg pattern? But Fi had done it this time. It had taken over two years, but she had finally found the right present to get her sister back for all the hideous gifts.

She placed the parcel down and adjusted the bow, taking a step back to admire her handiwork.

I don't understand why you want to give your sister an ugly present.

"Shh, you'll give it away." Fi shushed her familiar, even though no one else could hear her.

Humans. Cressida shook her head in despair. *I'll never understand you.*

Agatha reappeared with her drink. "You really shouldn't have."

"I know."

"Is it…?"

"What do you think?"

"Oh, I knew you'd got my hints about the new lawnmower. I can't believe you found it though, it's been sold out for weeks online."

Fi smiled and took a sip of her drink. She had packed the box so it might look like a remote lawnmower. Agatha was going to be so surprised when she saw her actual gift.

"I'd better go say hi to the others. Mort's just arrived."

Fi looked up and her heart did a small flip in her chest as she spotted the tall doctor. He did a strange dance move and Fi rushed over to help him avoid the evil chickens. Cluck Norris scratched one foot across the lawn as if about to charge.

"Shoo! Go on, shoo you demon cockerel!"

"Thanks, I thought I was a goner for a minute." Mort bent down and gave her a kiss. Fi blushed, still unused to public displays of affection or quite able to believe that he was still going out with her. Even after their disastrous trip to Cornwall that had ended with a fight with the piskie queen, and Fi's habit of playing video games well into the night. If anyone could put up with that, it must be love.

"How'd the surprise gift go down?"

Fi tipped her head towards the pile of presents. "She'll love it as much as I loved her last present."

Mort grimaced. "The socks?"

Fi nodded. Mort lifted the cuff of his jeans to reveal his own pair of ugly socks.

"Why are you wearing them?"

"It seemed nice to make a gesture…I still need your family to like me."

"They love you more than me."

Not surprising. He doesn't snore.

Fi glared at her familiar. The small dragon-like creature blinked up at her. "Why don't you go chase a chicken?"

Cressida didn't deign to reply and flounced off to the food table in search of some barbeque steaks.

"Nonsense, your family loves you–"

"Fiona! There you are. Did you bring the cake?"

Chapter 4

"It's in my car, Mrs Blair."

Fi's mum clacked her cane on the patio slabs. "I've told you, doctor, my name is Nell."

"And I've told you, my name is Mort, not 'doctor'."

Nell smiled then turned to Fi with a small frown on her face. "Where were you? The cake was meant to be here before the party started."

"It's here now. I'll go get it."

"No need, I'll go," Mort volunteered and headed back the way he'd come, leaving Fi and her mother alone.

"Good spread."

"Thank you, it was more work than you'd think to organise a potluck buffet."

"Isn't that the point of potluck? That people just bring whatever they like?"

Nell gave Fiona a look that said she clearly didn't understand the rigours of organising a party. "Sometimes I wonder if you're really my daughter. You can't just let people bring 'whatever they like'. What if everyone brings a dessert?"

"Sounds good to me."

"Really, Fi, be sensible. You need the right mix of mains and puddings and Neville wanted to barbeque something so I had to take that into account. And then there's the dietary needs." Nell gestured to a smaller table where some salads sat wilting in the warm afternoon sun. "Oh, hello, Steve, Glen. Put the kebabs over there would you?" Nell's eyes narrowed as she spotted the second Tupperware box in Steve's arms. "What's that?"

"Oh, I just thought I'd make some of those sugar cookies that Agatha likes. The ones with the sprinkles. Zadie helped."

"I made sure the zombies got the red sprinkles."

Fi took a step back. Steve and Glen's daughter was creepy enough when she wasn't talking about the undead.

"Yes, thank you Zadie. They're not all shaped like zombies, ha ha, we did some flowers too."

"Deadly nightshade."

"Thank you, Zadie, why don't we go say happy birthday to Agatha?" Glen wrapped an arm around his daughter and ushered her over to the birthday girl.

"I'll just, er, go and, er, help Mort," Fi said, rushing over to the gate and abandoning Steve to face her mother alone.

"Coward," he mouthed over her mum's shoulder as Nell bent to investigate the box. Fi gave an apologetic smile back.

It was a cowardly move, but she got enough disapproval from her mum already.

She held the gate open for Mort and guided him over to the display table. "Careful!"

"It's heavy."

"It's seven tiers, what did you expect?"

"There."

Fi winced as Mort pulled his arms out from under the behemoth sponge. It had taken her two solid days of online videos and more attempts than she could count at icing to get it right. But now, a perfect bouquet of butter icing roses cascaded down one side of the cake. Fi frowned. Was that peach rose a touch too big?

Mort kissed her on the top of her head. "It's perfect."

How did he know what she was thinking? "I should have spent more time on the icing. The pink one is too dark."

"It looks exactly like the rose over there. She'll love it."

"Hmmm." Nell appeared behind Fi, making her jump. "Where's the candle?"

"I didn't put one in."

"Hmmmf." Her mother marched off, her walking stick digging into the grass with every step. She returned a moment later with an enormous sparkler. "There," she said as she jammed the end into the middle tier.

Fi gaped. Her perfect icing. Ruined. "Mum!"

"No need to thank me." With that Nell turned away, her cane almost coming down on Fi's foot. Fi glared after her. She didn't even need that stupid stick anymore. Her leg was fully healed.

"Great cake. Did you make it?"

Fi turned and nodded at the stranger standing next to her. She wore a huge flouncy dress and a brightly coloured hat that matched it perfectly. Fi shuffled and wiped her hands on her skater style dress.

"I'm Hetty. I work with Agatha at the school."

"Fi, I'm her sister."

"Oh, I can see it now, you have the same eyes. Different hair, though."

Fi's hand went to her white hair. It was very different from her sister's glossy brown mane. But that was what happened when you channelled too much power, too quickly, without being ready for it. She pushed away the bad memories of that day before they could trap her in their spiralling web of self-hate. She could loathe herself tomorrow. Today was about her sister.

"So what do you teach?"

"Oh, no, I don't teach. I'm temping. I do the admin. Make sure everyone else is organised." The woman turned as someone else entered the garden. "Looks like Agatha invited everyone."

Fi followed her gaze to the wispy man draped in a black cloak. "Bit dramatic for a garden party."

"Oh he's always like that. Trying to look like he's all occult, it's not healthy to have such an obsession with the darker side of magic. I suppose I'd better go and say hi, otherwise he'll accuse me of ignoring him and I can't face one of his tantrums on Monday. See you later."

Agatha drifted over. "How was Hetty?"

"Hmmm? Oh fine."

"Good, good. It was awful how her son died so suddenly, I was a bit worried the party would be too much for her."

Fi watched the woman in the flowery dress say something to the bloke dressed from head to toe in black. "I think she's doing alright."

Agatha turned and waved at another guest. "I'd better do the rounds. Try to be friendly."

"I'm always…" Fi trailed off. Her sister had gone.

"Fiona!"

Fi turned to see a short teenager barrelling towards her. "Diane. Long time, no see."

"Yeah, look, I'm really sorry about all that stuff I did." She made a gesture as if nearly killing her friend was an inconsequential blip in the past. "But I'm learning loads. Look, I made this charm for Mrs Blair to say thank you, and I did one for you too. It's lucky."

Fi eyed the charm. It was shaped like a laptop, and looked like it was made out of metal. But the last time Diane had enchanted a piece of jewellery, it had almost killed someone.

"That's very…kind of you…but I don't wear jewellery."

"That's OK, it can go on your keyring." The girl pressed it into Fi's hand. It felt warm against her skin, but nothing else. "Please. I want to do something for you. I know you didn't have to recommend me for supervision instead of prison. It's safe. My teacher tested it."

She waved over and to Fi's horror, the cloak wearer began to walk towards them. The man's face was tight and he looked like he'd never smiled in his life. Fi found herself caught by his eyes, so dark they were almost black, with a ring of gold around the irises. He held out a limp hand to Fi and winced when she shook it.

"Quentin Lenoir, at your service."

"Hi Quentin, I'm Fi. Diane was just telling me about her charms."

"Ah, so you're the tech witch. Diane has high praise for you. I would be interested in seeing your powers in action."

Fi shivered. There was something about his words that sounded creepy as heck. In response to her fear, her powers sparked under her skin, ready to leap to the surface and protect her. Fi kept them locked down. She was not going to ruin her sister's party by being too jumpy.

Cressida darted over, flowing across the lawn in a streak of gold. She dropped a sausage on the grass and ran her forked tongue over her teeth.

What's happening? I can sense your fear. Who harmed you?

"Er, this is my familiar, Cressida." Fi bent down and pocketed the sausage. "Calm down," she whispered to her anxious familiar.

Who is this?

"Cressida, meet Quentin, Diane's new teacher."

"A wyrm, fascinating…and I take it you have a psychic bond with her? How unusual. You are certainly a witch of unique talents."

Fi shifted her feet, uncomfortable under Quentin's stare. She felt like an animal in a lab, waiting to be jabbed with needles for an experiment.

"Mr Lenoir, tell her that the charms are safe for her to wear." Diane turned her large eyes to her supervisor, forcing his gaze from Fi.

He blinked in surprise. "Of course, they are, I tested them myself. Diane is rather adept at infusing items with magic. She has spent the entire month practising her luck infusions."

Fi forced a smile. The fact that Mr Creepy had tested them didn't reassure her, but she couldn't feel anything malicious from the charm, so she looped it on her keyring. "Thanks Diane, I could use all the luck I can get."

"Really?" Quentin eyed her. "Why is that?"

"Oh, er, just this latest case."

"Fi's amazing. She works for the Magical Liaison Office. What's the case?"

Fi looked to the sky for help. A small cloud skated past, but no inspiration fell from the sky. She chickened out. How could she explain that she was under suspicion for murder to a teenager? "I can't say. Top secret."

"Fascinating," said Quentin again. Fi had never known a word to sound so fear inducing.

"Fi!"

She whipped her head round and smiled gratefully at Liv, gliding across the patio.

"Liv! Sorry, I'd better go say hi. Great to see you, Diane, I'm really glad you're doing well." And she was. The girl had been trouble, learning her magic without focus, but she seemed settled now, growing in confidence. "Lovely to meet you, too, Quentin," she lied.

"Likewise."

He was…odd.

"Agreed," Fi said under her breath as she scurried off to see Liv.

Chapter 5

"Great cake."

"Thanks. Took me forever, but I think Aggy'll like it. You look…amazing." It was true. Liv's skin glowed and her hair shone in the afternoon sun. Her relaxed off the shoulder dress had heads turning across the garden, not that Liv took any notice of the attention. "I take it you had a great time at the spa."

"It was a wellness retreat."

"Same difference."

Liv eyed her. "You should try it some time."

Fi considered it. "A week on my own…sounds good. What's the wifi signal like?"

Liv burst out laughing, causing several men to turn in her direction. She wiped away a tear. "There's no wifi. The point is to disconnect from everything and focus on yourself."

Cressida snorted. *You couldn't last five minutes without checking your phone.*

Fi shuddered. Why would someone want to put themselves through that? "Sounds awful."

"So, do you think Agatha invited the entire town?"

"Seems that way." Fi returned the waves of Jack, Jeremy and Harris, who sat sprawling on a garden bench instead of their usual spot outside the Witch's Brew pub. The trio had old-fashioned jug style pint glasses in their hands and seemed content to watch the party from their new spot. Jeremy had even put a jumper over his string vest for the occasion.

"Who's that? He seems familiar…" Fi eyed a man helping himself to a large sausage in a bun.

"I think he runs the charity shop on the High Street."

"Right." That explained why she recognised him. She'd interviewed him as part of her investigations into the malicious enchanted items…the ones Diane had infused with mischievous magic. Was there anyone her sister hadn't invited?

"Where's Valentine?"

"He'll be here later, once the sun's lower." That was one part of the vampire myth that was true; they didn't like the sun.

Fi's mum tapped a spoon against a glass. The delicate tinkle rang over the garden, far louder than it should have been thanks to her mum's magic. Even the bees quieted their buzzing. Everybody turned to where she floated gently in front of the table of presents.

"I wanted to thank you all for making the time to come to my daughter's birthday party. It's wonderful to see so many familiar faces from the village. Now, manners forbid me from saying her age, but let's just say it's a testament to her excellent nature that she has so many friends."

"Oh goddess, this isn't a WWWI event, why is she giving a speech?" Fi rolled her eyes at her mother's antics. She supposed that her mum just couldn't help herself. Speeches and wanting to be centre of attention came with the territory as Chair of the local branch of the Wizards', Witches' and Warlocks' Institute.

Agatha smiled politely from the side, but Fi could tell from her flushed face and the way she gripped her glass that her sister was dying of embarrassment. She looked around and saw Bea skipping over by a flowerbed. Perfect. As her mother droned on, Fi sidled up to her niece.

"Hey Bumble Bea."

"Aunty Fi, look at this flower."

"Very pretty…"

"It's a perfect specimen of *digitalis purpurea* and the *helianthus annus* is growing well."

Fi blinked. Definitely her sister's daughter. "Sure, and do you know who'd love to see it? Your granny. Why don't you run over and give her a hug?"

Bea plucked the flower and barrelled through the crowd before launching herself at Nell. Just in time. She'd started talking about Agatha's birth and Fi could almost hear her sister willing the ground to open up and swallow her. Fi followed the path through the guests her niece had carved and took a spot near the present table.

"Bea, Granny's talking. Yes, that's a lovely flower."

"Presents! Mummy – look at all your presents."

Fi smiled. Trust a child to care more about presents than speeches.

Her mother coughed. "Yes, well I'm sure you've all put a lot of thought into your gifts, so perhaps you should open them now so you can thank people in person, Agatha."

"I don't know…" Agatha said.

"You have to open them now, Mummy! It's your birthday party!"

"Go on, Aggy," Fi added her voice to the pleas, a glint in her blue eyes.

"Alright," Agatha smiled. She wiped her hands on her corduroy jeans and picked up a small box wrapped in shiny gold paper. "This is from Neville and Bea. Thank you."

"Just open it, Mummy."

Agatha unwrapped the paper and gasped as she opened a jewellery box to reveal a charm bracelet. Neville fastened it around her plump wrist with a smile and she kissed him.

Fi pretended to gag.

"Come on, it's sweet," Mort said, wrapping an arm around her waist.

"Not when it's your sister."

"And this is from Mort."

Fi's eyes shot up to her boyfriend. He shrugged. "I thought she might appreciate it."

Agatha unwrapped the paper to reveal a pair of stripy, fluffy socks. "I love them! Thank you."

Mort looked confused. Fi stifled a laugh. If he thought bad fashion sense would phase her sister, he was wrong. She'd seen her in her wedding dress, and tweed and lace was an interesting combination. Neville whispered something in Agatha's ear and her sister blushed and swatted his hand away from her waist. Ugh. Fi looked away.

Agatha unwrapped each of her gifts, one by one, pausing to hug her party guests and thank them as the pile of scarves and gardening equipment grew on the table. Fi tapped her foot as she waited for her sister to open her present, but Agatha seemed determined to leave it for last. Finally, it was the only box left.

"And now, this one is from my darling sister."

Fi snapped her head back and grinned.

"I wonder what it could be…" Agatha tore open the flowery wrapping paper and pulled back the cardboard underneath to reveal an ugly gnome. The vilest one that Fi had been able to find. The gnome had a dumpy face that would have looked better on a gargoyle, twisted into a lurid grimace beneath its sparse carved beard that had made Fi stop when she'd seen it outside the garden centre. A traditional pointed hat topped its wispy hair, and the sculptor had painted its clothes so it would be centre of attention wherever it was placed in the garden. It sported a bright green top and carnelian red trousers above boots in a shade that could only rightly be called 'dog poo brown'.

"Oh. It's er…"

"Don't you love him? I've named him Gnomeo and I know he'll look great in your garden."

"Oh, yes, the garden…"

"Maybe…here?" Fi picked up the offensive gnome and strode to the centre of Agatha's manicured lawn where an antique birdbath provided a tasteful touch to the garden.

Agatha hurried behind her sister. "Oh, I'm not sure about that, it's so bright…maybe it would be better in a flower bed."

"Where no one can see him?" Fi pretended to look hurt.

"Well…"

"Great." Fi placed him on the ground in front of the birdbath and grinned. She'd hit Agatha where it hurt; in her garden. The perfect payback for all the tasteless presents she'd had to endure over the years. The knee-high gnome drew every eye.

"That's certainly… something." Fi heard someone in the crowd say.

"Won't lose him, for sure," said one of the trio on the bench.

"You'll see that shirt from space!"

Agatha gave her sister a weak smile and turned back to her guests. "I think it's time to cut the cake."

Fi beamed. This couldn't have gone better. She stayed next to her gnome while Agatha bustled off to the cake.

"Remind me never to get on your bad side," Mort said, appearing at her shoulder.

She patted his arm. "Just don't ever get me a dodgy gift and I won't."

"Speaking of gifts…"

Fi raised an eyebrow as Mort reached inside his jacket. An explosion made them both turn. Fi's mouth dropped open in horror.

"Sorry everyone, I must have overdone the magic." Behind Nell, the sparkler continued to spray sparks fifty feet up in the air as everyone ran for cover. The firework amped up its display with a bang, sending cake splattering over the garden. With a flick of her wrist, Nell sent a jet of water at the firework, causing it to fizz and sputter in protest.

Fi stared as the remains of her carefully crafted iced roses melted down the side of the cake.

Fi's mouth moved, but she couldn't find the words to express how much time, effort and love she'd put into this masterpiece for Agatha, because, as much as she wanted to get her back for her questionable taste in gifts, she did love her sister.

I don't know what all the fuss is about, it's only cake.

Fi made a noise somewhere between a sob and a groan. Mort put his arm around her, and she rested against the reassuring warmth of his body.

Will you take a picture of me?

"What for?"

My followers love to see me at sunset. The light is perfect.

Typical. All Fi's hard work on the cake had been destroyed and her familiar was more concerned about posing. "I knew it was a mistake putting you on Instagram."

Fi took out her phone and snapped a few pictures. Say what you want about Cressida – and Fi frequently had a few choice words for her – but the golden wyrm was photogenic.

Get my good side.

Fi felt Mort tense and look around next to her.

"Sorry, got to go. Be back soon." With that, he withdrew his arm and headed for the shed.

Fi stared after him, her mouth widening as she spotted the swirling black portal opening next to her sister's potting shed. "Sorry, Cress. Now's not the time for pictures."

Chapter 6

Mort stepped through the portal without a second's hesitation.

Fi swore and raced across the garden. Like heck she was letting her boyfriend go through a strange portal on his own. She called her magic to her hands and dived through before it shut behind her with a faint buzz.

Air hit Fi's face as she fell through a dark night sky, stars rushed past, blurring into streaks of white. Fi hit the ground with a thud. She rubbed her head and looked around.

Mort knelt on the grey stone, his right hand crossed over his heart and his head bent. Fi closed her eyes and opened them again. She wasn't mistaken. Floating in a void in front of him was a gigantic skull.

The bone was a pale white and swept up into ridged horns that curved back and around, almost like a ram's skull. The eye sockets glowed with a green light. It gave off a sense of power that made Fi sink to her knees. Whatever it was, the skull was full of ancient magic. She didn't need to dampen her own power down to sense that.

WHO DARES TO ENTER MY REALM WITHOUT MY PERMISSION?

Fi looked around. The words entered her head in a deep, echoing voice that reverberated inside her mind without going through her ears. The skull was talking to her. And it expected some sort of reply. "Er, hi. I'm Fiona, Fiona Blair, but you can call me Fi."

"Fi! What are you doing here?"

"I followed you through the portal." Fi twisted her toes into the ground. She shouldn't have followed Mort.

WHO IS THIS MORTAL?

"She's my girlfriend, this is all a mistake. She bears no responsibility, let me take her back to the mortal realm." There was an edge of panic to his voice that Fi hadn't heard before.

"Mort? What's going on?"

MORTIMER GREGORIUS DE'ATH IS ON TRIAL FOR SUBVERSION OF THE NATURAL ORDER.

She crawled on her knees until she was in front of Mort, forcing herself to look at the huge skull. "He didn't do anything wrong. I know him, he'd never do anything to subvert the natural order. You've made a mistake."

"Fi, please."

GODS DO NOT MAKE MISTAKES. BUT I SENSE YOU ALSO HAVE A PART IN THIS.

A god? Fi took a step backwards, pressing against Mort. So this was Arawn, God of Death and Mort's master.

"Let me take her back."

YOU WILL BEAR FULL RESPONSIBILITY FOR THE TRANSFER OF SOULS?

"Transfer of souls? What's he talking about? Wait…you mean Effie, don't you? What's happening here?"

MORTIMER DECIDED TO SAVE THE SOUL OF OPHELIA HARRINGTON INSTEAD OF LETTING HER DIE, AS IS THE NATURAL ORDER.

"But, he had to. Her sister had killed people, he couldn't let her back in her body." Fi garbled the words, knowing that they didn't make any sense.

I AM UNCONCERNED WITH MORTAL SINS, ONLY WITH THE NATURAL ORDER.

"What happens if he's found guilty?"

HE WILL FACE A TEST.

Fi bit her lip.

"Fi, please, you have to go back. Let me take her back." Mort's voice rose in panic. "It's not safe for you."

"And it is for you? I'm not leaving." Fi crossed her arms and eyed the skull. "You'll have to put both of us on trial. I was the one who wouldn't let it go. I made Liv go to the dream realm. It was all my idea."

YOU SPEAK THE TRUTH.

"No! No, it was me. Only me. She has nothing to do with this."

YOU CARE FOR THIS MORTAL.

Mort hung his head and nodded. Fi squeezed his hand. It wasn't the best declaration of love he'd ever made, and he seemed more upset about it than happy right now, but she wasn't leaving him alone to face this stupid test. Wasn't that love? Sticking with someone through the good times and the bad, and you couldn't get much worse than facing down the God of Death together. She stuck her chin out.

AND SHE INSISTS THAT SHE BEARS THE BLAME. Fi swallowed. The green eyes dimmed a little, as if the skull were thinking. I HAVE DECIDED. YOU SHALL BOTH FACE THE TEST. IF YOU PASS, I WILL DEEM YOU WORTHY AS MY SERVANTS IN THE MORTAL PLANE.

"And if we don't?"

THEN THE MORTAL REALM WILL NO LONGER BE OF CONCERN.

"You mean, we'll die?" Fi frowned. That didn't seem fair. She opened her mouth to protest, but the stone shook under her feet and she toppled to one side, her hand wrenching free of Mort's. Walls broke through the earth, splitting the dark grey stone and towering high above her.

"Mort?" she screamed.

"I'm here, Fi," he shouted back.

YOU MUST FIND EACH OTHER BEFORE THE TIME ELAPSES TO COMPLETE THE TEST.

An hourglass the size of a house appeared in the night sky above their head. It glowed with a wispy green light as it turned over in the air. Sand that glittered like the stars trickled through the hole in the centre. The test had begun.

Chapter 7

"Mort! What can you see?"

"Nothing. Just the wall. You stay there, and I'll try to find you."

Fi looked down the corridor. Faint wisps of mist curled between the huge stone walls, lending a whiter shade of grey to the lack of colour in the labyrinth. A growl sounded far to her left.

"I'm not sure staying still is an option. There's something else in here."

"OK, which way are you going?"

"Right. Definitely right."

"I'll go that way too. Keep talking so we can find each other. And try to keep one hand on the wall, so you don't get lost."

Fi trailed her right hand on the smooth wall. It didn't feel like rock, it felt smoother and cold to touch, like black glass. Fi shivered. It felt unwelcoming and chilled her, not just at her fingertips but somewhere deep inside her soul.

"Fi? Are you still there?"

"Yep."

"Keep talking."

The English language flew out of her head as she struggled to think of something to say. "The Konami code was first used in Gradius on the NES."

There was a long moment of silence from the other side.

"Mort?"

"What was that?"

"I panicked."

"What's the can-o-mi code?"

"Konami. It's a cheat code; up, up, down, down, left, right, left, right, B, A, Start. It's in practically every video game, but it started because the game designer for Gradius wanted an easier way to test the game, so he put in the code to give him all the power ups early on."

More silence.

"You said to keep talking."

"You're right. Hang on, there's a turning up here. Can you still hear me?" Mort's voice became quieter.

"Yes, just. You tell me something."

"I tell everyone I became a doctor to help people, but really a big part of it was because my Dad was a doctor. I seem to have spent my life following in his footsteps…"

"I thought you liked being a doctor?" A turning loomed in front of Fi. With no other option, she turned right.

"I do," Mort's voice was fainter now. "But, Dad was a great doctor until he retired."

"You're a great doctor! You knew I was lying the first time I came to see you."

Mort's laugh vanished into a cry of fear. Fi pressed both hands against the wall, straining her ears to hear. "Mort? Mort?!"

Was that a growl? The scuttle of feet? "Mort! What's happening?"

With no answer, she sped up. A creak echoed through the corridor. "Mort?"

A growl behind her sent a shiver down her spine. Fi ran. Footsteps pounded behind her. The echo of her own racing steps or something else? She swallowed and kept going. Another corner. No choices. She sprinted on, her feet slipping on the ground as she raced around the corner.

Why didn't she listen to Cressida when her familiar told her to exercise?

Fi skidded to a stop, clutching the stitch in her side. A large shadow loomed in front of her. Fi pressed tight against the freezing wall, holding her breath. The shadow sniffed, its dark tongue flicking out to taste the air. Behind her, Fi heard the scurry of footsteps. So, whatever followed her was scared of this creature. Great. Fi took a step backwards. The creature's head snapped towards her.

It wore a long cloak of shadow that rippled in greys and blacks as it swirled around the creature as if caught in a breeze. A hood covered the top half of its face. But the bottom half was terrifying enough. Its pointed teeth jutted out from between dry, grey lips and its nose was a bump with two narrow slits, like a snake.

It darted forward. Fi closed her eyes, bracing for impact. She felt a rush of air, but nothing more. She slitted one eye open. The creature was level with her. It tilted its head back and forth, scenting the air. It couldn't see, Fi realised. She kept still. It moved on, gliding slowly, the only sound a breath of air as its tongue darted back and forth.

It was almost on her now, its head so close she could see the peeling skin. Fi gathered her power beneath her skin, afraid to loose it in case the thing could sense magic.

A roar sounded far away in the labyrinth. The creature's head snapped up and it floated up to the top of the wall. Fi took her chance. She sprinted down the corridor.

The thing gave a rattle of annoyance that froze Fi's blood, but she forced herself on, running through the pain in her muscles as they protested at the sudden exercise. The hairs on the back of her neck pricked up as she felt its cool breath on her skin.

Fi urged her legs to run faster, ploughing depths of energy she didn't know she possessed to escape the creature. She felt the pull of fabric as a skeletal hand reached out and grasped at her dress. She swatted at it and yanked the material away.

Another turning. She dashed around it. The creature choked off another rattle. Panting, she slowed, her body unable to maintain the breakneck speed. She pressed her back against the wall and spun, ready to fight what she couldn't outrun. But it was no longer within a hair's breadth of her. Instead, it hovered in the corner where the walls joined, snapping forward then retreating and hissing at her with bared yellow teeth.

It couldn't get beyond its part of the maze. The thought raced across Fi's mind. But why? Where was the logic in that? Unless there were more monsters and each had its own section…Fi shuddered as she gulped oxygen into her lungs.

She weighed her options. Go ahead into the unknown or go back the way she'd come. The creature gnashed its teeth and strained against whatever invisible restraint held it in its section. Go forward. Away from that…thing.

"Mort?" It came out like a gasp. No reply. She looked up at the glowing hourglass. Half the time had already gone and she'd turned two corners. Fi inhaled, braced herself against the obsidian wall and moved on.

Chapter 8

Fi decided that the best way to speed up was to slow down. She spent precious seconds reaching out with her magic, trying to sense the tiny electrical pulses emitted by living creatures. It was a new skill and one she wasn't adept at. Her heart drummed against her ribs. Nothing. She squinted down the dark corridor. She couldn't see anything either.

Fi walked on. She turned the corner and stopped. Fi stared up and up at the enormous beast blocking the corridor. Three heads stared down from atop its huge hairy black body. Its paws were the size of a table and thudded on the ground as it squared off against her.

"Cerberus?"

The massive hound wagged its tail at its name, but all three heads pulled their lips back to bare their huge teeth.

"Woah, there. I don't mean any harm."

Three huge noses sniffed the air. Fi scrabbled back and something stretched against her thigh in her jeans. She put her hand in her pocket and brought out a sausage. Fi stared at it, then held it out to the dog. Six orange eyes focused on the small sausage and strands of saliva poured from three gaping maws.

The middle head snatched up the offering, the others growling and whining as it chomped on the meat.

"Good boy."

Cerberus nuzzled her, almost knocking her from her feet. It whined. Fi could have laughed. The dog looked like a huge version of Mort's dad's dog. If that canine had three heads.

"Sorry, boy, I don't have any more."

The huge dog upped the whining.

"I said I don't have any more, but if you could let me pass, that'd be awesome."

The three giant heads stared down at her and cocked to one side in unison. Long strings of drool dangled from its mouth.

The head she had fed nuzzled her again, but the other two growled.

"Er, Cerby? Everything OK?"

The large head nudged her backwards, then snapped its teeth at the other heads. Fi stared between them, backing up as the middle head and the left hand one got into a biting match.

The head on the right kept its orange eyes on her, teeth bared. Its growl shuddered through her.

"Easy there." She held her hands up, trying to de-escalate things.

The right head lunged forward, teeth bared. Fi launched a lightning bolt at the attacking head and the smell of singed fur surrounded her. Cerberus yelped and the right head fell to the ground with a thunk. The middle head whined, and turned its puppy dog eyes on her.

"Sorry, boy."

The left head growled and darted forward, its left paw moving with it. The right-hand side flopped, immobile along with the right head. Fi sidestepped and aimed another blast of electricity at the enormous hound.

The left head rolled to one side and hit the wall, its pink tongue lolling out of its enormous mouth as it slumped down the black obsidian to the floor.

The middle head snorted and whined again, settling down between the two other heads. It gazed at Fi with huge eyes, and she stretched out a hand and ruffled its fur. It closed its eyes and a deep snore rumbled from inside its chest.

Fi backed away as its doggy breath fluttered the loose strands of hair around her face. "I think I just knocked them out. They'll come around later. Sorry, boy."

She clambered over the dormant dog and raced on through the never-ending corridors. Was that someone shouting?

"Mort?"

"Fi?" His voice was faint but there. He was close.

"Mort! I'm close."

"Fi, I don't…I can't…I don't know how to get to you." She heard thumping on the wall and banged her own fists on the unforgiving black glass. She sank to the floor, her back against the wall and a dry sob racked her body.

There had to be a better way than fighting monsters. She had no idea how large the labyrinth was or how to get to Mort, even if he sounded close. Fi dug the heels of her hands into her eyes. They were both going to die. If only there was a way she could get above the walls and find him.

A crazy idea flashed through her head. She looked up at the trickling star sand leaking through the hourglass. Time was running out and it was the only idea she had.

She swallowed and ran back the way she'd come. Time for something crazy.

Chapter 9

Fi climbed over the stunned Cerberus, holding her breath at the stench of its dog breath. She scooped up one of its gnawed bones, screwing her face up at the dried flesh still clinging to the white bone, and jogged back down the corridor. She hoped this would work.

Fi paused at the corner and pressed herself up against the stone wall. She peeked round. The creature was there, back in its place. It made a rattling sound as it paced back and forth, protecting its territory. Fi swallowed hard. She had barely escaped it the first time, now she was going back for more. *I must be mad.* But mad was what Fi needed right now. She took three deep breaths. It had to work.

Fi swung her arm and threw the bone down the corridor. It bounced off the rock with a clatter that made the creature spin round. It sniffed then flew at the fleshy remnants of whatever poor soul the bone had belonged to, a grinding screeching noise swirled around the labyrinth as its sharp teeth chewed down.

She bounced onto her toes and sped forwards as quietly as she could. Two paces away, it paused its horrific eating and sniffed. Fi collided with it and hugged her arms around its brittle neck. It screamed and weaved back and forth, trying to shake her off.

Fi wrapped her legs around its skinny body and held on tight as it hissed its displeasure and dug at her skin with its bony fingers. She gritted her teeth and tightened her grip, ignoring the scratches to her arm. Above them, the glowing sand continued to fall.

The creature jerked back, slamming Fi against the hard wall. Her head collided with the stone, and she shifted her grip, yanking at the creature's neck.

"Up!"

It screeched and flew upwards, zig zagging between the narrow walls of the corridor. Every bump shook Fi to her core, but she clung on. This was her only chance. Then it was above the wall, screaming its horrible high-pitched cry.

Fi judged the distance, swallowed hard and launched herself off of the writhing beast. She flailed and swore as she flew towards the wall. It smacked into her chest with a thump that reverberated across the maze. Fi swore again. It came out as a breath of air. Winded, she hugged the top of the cool stone, marvelling that she had made it and was still alive.

Behind her, the creature screamed as it crashed into the opposite wall, forced into the rock thanks to the momentum of her jump. Fi did a speedy crabwalk away from the monster, trying to put as much distance between her and it before it recovered.

It hissed as it righted itself and sped towards her. Fi pushed herself to her feet and increased her speed, her eyes focused on the right angle in the wall up ahead. The spot that marked the end of its territory. She had to make it.

A skeletal hand grabbed at her ankle, and she smashed against the top of the wall. Fi kicked out with the other foot, clenching her jaw at the jarring impact with the rock. The creature's cry ran down her spine like a cold glass of water. The grip loosened and she kicked again, staggering to her feet.

She was so close. Fi stumbled forward. The thing recovered again. Its hissing breath filled her ears in a strange duet with her smashing heartbeat. She looked back and jumped to avoid its grasp. Less than two metres now. But it was right behind her.

With a cry, she jumped across the corner, hitting the intersecting wall with a dull thud. The air rushed out of her lungs and she gripped the squared off rock, her feet scrabbling against the sheer wall before she pulled herself up.

She lay there, staring up at the hourglass still counting down, giving herself precious seconds to swallow air, before she got up.

The creature, whatever demon it was, bared its teeth at her and reached out with its yellowed claws, but it couldn't touch her. Fi stuck out her tongue in a fit of petulance, sudden elation filling her. She wasn't dead. Not yet.

"Mort!" she yelled across the labyrinth.

"Fi?"

She scanned the maze. From her perch, she could see that the walls seemed to go on forever, passing the horizon of her vision, but there was some sort of pattern. If she had time, maybe she could work it out, but for now, she had to find her lover.

A disturbance in the wispy white fog that filled the corridors and gave some dim light to the maze caught her eye. Mort. She ran along the top of the wall, keeping her eyes fixed on the swirling mist, not allowing her mind to wander to the steep drop on either side of her.

When she was level with the cloud, she slowed, coming to a careful stop before crouching down. He was three corridors across. Fi glanced left and right. Endless corridors, with their abrupt turns, spread out on either side with no clear way to get to him.

Only one thing for it then. Fi judged the distance and leapt, arms outstretched. She hung in the air, then collided with the opposite wall. How many times could one knock the air out of their lungs before causing permanent damage? Fi hoped she'd live to find out, because she was still two jumps away.

"Mort, I'm coming," she wheezed. The sound of metal clashing with stone rang around the labyrinth. He was in trouble.

Fi swallowed down the dry retches that her body demanded and braced herself for the next jump. This time, she tensed, and the impact didn't feel so hard, or maybe she was used to the sensation now. Her body so bruised that it couldn't acknowledge anymore damage. Was that a thing? Mort would know.

Last jump. Fi stood and took a deep breath before leaping over the gap. Her momentum took her to the wall, but this time she misjudged. She landed hard, clacking her jaw against the stone. Dazed, her fingers slipped away from the edge. She kicked her feet hard, her rubber soles gripping the sheer wall. Fi tensed her elbows and her bruised jaw, using every ounce of burning muscle to pull herself up. Panting, she made it and collapsed onto the harsh stone.

"Mort, I'm here."

Chapter 10

She had to repeat herself twice before Mort heard. He stared up and his jaw dropped.

"Fi? What are you doing up there?"

"Getting to you."

Mort flew into a wall, his sword dropping to the ground with a clang as a huge snake took advantage of his lapse in concentration. It looped its thick body around him and squeezed. The sound of bone cracking rang through the air.

"Oh no you don't, snakey."

Fi jumped again, landing on its triangular head more by accident than aim. She clung on as it flailed beneath her. She called her magic to her palms and let her electricity flow into the giant reptile. It coiled in on itself in agony, twisting and turning. Mort cried out and Fi slid down its smooth scales to where he was trapped. She pulled at the constricting coils, but the quivering muscles didn't move.

"I found you," she said. Fi turned her head to the sky. So few grains of sand still swirled in the hourglass. "I found him!" she shouted. "Stop the test! I found him!"

No answer came from the star spattered sky. "I found you," she sobbed, gazing into Mort's chocolate brown eyes. Didn't gods keep their bargains? It wasn't fair. She reached out and cupped his pain-streaked face. At least they were together at the end.

As soon as her fingers touched his face, the ginormous snake vanished and both Mort and Fi dropped to the floor. The walls melted back into the ground and the mist cleared. Arawn's enormous skull face appeared in front of them.

YOU HAVE PASSED THE TEST.

"That's it? He almost died!" Fi stood, shaking with anger. "Why didn't you stop the test when I found him?"

I DID.

Fi opened her mouth to shout again, but Mort grasped her hand. She gazed down at him, and he shook his head. "It's not worth it, trust me."

Fi stared at him. How could he be so blasé? How many times had he endured something like this for his master? She squeezed his hand.

"So what happens now?"

YOU HAVE PASSED THE TEST SO YOU ARE WORTHY TO CONTINUE AS MY EMISSARY IN THE MORTAL REALM.

With a blink of his neon eyes, the pain in Fi's chest and legs disappeared. Mort stood, panting, but the grimace of pain had left his face. He bowed his head to the god.

AND I HAVE A TASK FOR YOU.

Fi made a noise somewhere between a snort and a spit. "A task, that's rich." She was running on adrenaline, that was the only answer she could come up with. That's what she told herself later when she replayed the moment that she talked back to a dzraking god.

A TASK FOR BOTH OF YOU.

Fi's mouth dropped open.

COMPLETE THE TASK AND, AS A GESTURE OF THANKS TO YOU BOTH, I SHALL GRANT YOU A BOON. NEVER LET IT BE SAID THAT I AM A CRUEL MASTER.

"And if we fail?" Fi couldn't help herself. Clearly her common sense had got knocked out of her when she cracked her head.

IF YOU FAIL, THEN IT IS LIKELY YOU SHALL DIE.

Brilliant.

"What is the task you require of me, great Arawn?" Mort stepped forward, placing himself between Fi and the floating skull.

THERE IS A NECROMANCER AT WORK IN THE MORTAL REALM CLOSE TO WHERE YOU ARE BASED. I CHARGE YOU TO STOP THEM.

"Wait, a necromancer? As in someone who raises the dead?"

A MAGIC USER WHO SUBVERTS THE NATURAL ORDER AND ROBS MY REALM OF PEACE.

"I will take on this task," Mort said, bowing his head.

YOU ARE BOTH WORTHY. YOU WILL BOTH COMPLETE THIS TASK FOR ME.

With that, the skull faded from view, the bright green eyes lingering a moment after until they too paled into the night sky. A swirling portal opened behind them with a sucking noise. Mort pulled Fi through before he whirled to face her. "What were you thinking?"

"I beg your pardon?" She staggered to the side, trying to orient herself after the portal travel. They were in the cellar under Mort's house. Fi recognised the stone floor and slight damp smell that came with any underground cellar.

"Antagonising a god, Fi." She snapped her attention to her boyfriend. He ran his fingers through his hair. "Why did you come here in the first place?"

"I saw you walk through an evil portal, forgive me for wanting to help."

"I had it covered. I made the decision to place Effie's soul in another body. I should have been the one to face the consequences. Instead, you barrel in and…" he grabbed her arm, "…and you could have been killed. Because of me." His voice broke into a sob.

"Mort," she said softly, "I'm OK. And we're a team, remember. I'm not going to let you face the God of Death on your own, even if he is your master. I do have one question though…"

"Yes?"

"Is your middle name really Gregorius?"

"Is yours really Joules?"

Chapter 11

Mort shook his head and led them out of the cellar to the main part of the house. He paused in the kitchen to put the kettle on, while Fi retrieved two mugs from a cupboard.

"Any idea how we find this necromancer?"

Mort shook his head. "I know as much as you."

Fi huffed out a breath. "I'll check the MLO database and see if there are any reports, but he said the necromancer was close to us and I haven't heard anything about raising the dead."

"Thanks Fi, I appreciate it. Maybe it'll be fun to work together again. After all we made a good team tracking down the queen of the piskies and stopping her mischief."

"Fun's one word for it…" Mort had ended up injured and Fi had got severe burns when she channelled lightning to destroy the entrance to Joan the Wad's realm, but it had been a nice holiday.

Mort laughed. "Come on, admit it, we make a good team. In fact, there's something I've been wanting to ask–" Mort's hand went to his jacket pocket.

"There you are! Thought I felt someone come through the portal. What did old Arawn want now? Oh, hello Fi, how are you? Where's Cressida? Rus has been pining for his playmate." On cue, the old, jowly dog waddled into the room.

"Hi Hades," Fi greeted Mort's elderly father, careful to avoid the drip hooked into his arm. "She's at my sister's party. I'd better get back, actually."

"Not before you tell me all about your trip to the underworld. Did Mort show you the Elysian Fields?"

"It wasn't a date, Dad."

"Nonsense, why else would you take someone to the other realm?"

"Arawn summoned me." Mort glanced at Fi.

"I tagged along."

Hades let out a bark of laughter. "Bet that was a shock! I almost wet myself the first time I was in his presence. Tell me, what did he make of that? Serve him right to get a surprise every now and then. He sprung enough on me when I was younger. Did I ever tell you about the time I had to get a roebuck back into the other world? Took me almost a decade to track it down and it did not want to go, let me tell you." The old man pointed to a white scar on his neck.

"Dad. He gave us a task."

The smile on Hades' face fell away and his forehead creased with concern. "Us? Both of you?" He looked between Mort and Fi.

She nodded, confirming it.

The man sucked in a whistling breath through his teeth. "He must think you're something special then, girl. But we already knew you had to be if Mort chose you. What's this task, then? Can't be any more difficult than fighting the black toad. It took part of me into the other world with it." He held up a hand, and waggled his remaining fingers, emphasising the missing middle one.

"There's a necromancer…"

The old man swore. "That's bad. Not something I've come across myself. Escaped souls or beasts I could help you with, but this… I'll look in the books, see if any of our ancestors faced one."

"You keep records?"

"Of course. Our family's served Arawn for generations. They wrote down everything they could to help the next generation. Of course, most of it's in old English or Welsh and it's not always coherent or in any order and our handwriting isn't always legible. Probably why we make good doctors, hey?" He nudged his son in the ribs. "Anyway, one of our relatives copied it all out in the eighteenth century after we lost three volumes in a fire. My great-grandad tried to index it all, but it's not pretty. Want to have a look?"

Fi nodded and followed Mort's dad as he shuffled along to a room Fi hadn't seen before. He opened the door with a flourish.

"Here you go. No food or drink, perfect humidity levels. Everything to preserve the De'ath family library."

Fi stepped in after him and stared. It wasn't as impressive as the library at her mother's house but it was good enough. A wall lined with neat, leather bound books on wonky bookshelves faced the doorway.

"This is all the copied stuff. But in here…these are the originals." Hades turned a key in a locked cabinet and pulled open the dark wooden door to reveal scrolls and sheaves of paper. "We De'aths weren't always the best record keepers and the writing is terrible. Take a look." He handed Fi a scroll and she unfurled it carefully, feeling like she should wear protective gloves.

Spidery writing scrawled across the page, interspersed with fat blobs of ink. She squinted. Nope, she couldn't make out a single word.

"You can read this?"

"Not without a glass of whisky! You get used to it, but luckily we don't have to consult the originals often, it's all here in the reprints."

He plucked a book off the shelf. Fi braced herself for a shudder of disapproval from the house, before remembering that she wasn't in a magic house that only allowed you to take the books it offered from its shelves. He flicked it open and passed it to Fi.

She nodded at the neatly printed text.

"It's a bit long winded, more so than the originals, but it works. If we have anything on necromancers, I'll find it. Fancy helping?"

"I really should get back to Cressida and it's my sister's birthday."

"In that case, take her a present from me." He shuffled back into the hall with surprising speed for a man hooked up to an IV drip. Seconds later he returned and pressed a box into Fi's hand.

"What is it?"

"A gift from the other world."

"Dad! You shouldn't just give those out."

"What? If I want to give some old apple seeds as gifts, I will. And if she can get them to grow, then she deserves them."

"Thank you?"

Hades nodded and turned back to the books. Mort walked Fi to the door, but she held up a hand to his chest. "You should stay and help your dad. I'll get back to the party before someone raises the alarm."

He frowned. "OK. Will you come over later?"

"I should probably check out the database. I'll message you." Fi slunk away without looking back.

Chapter 12

It was a coward's move and Fi berated herself the entire walk to her sister's house. But Mort's cryptic question that he'd tried to ask twice now thudded around her mind. He couldn't want to marry her, could he?

They hadn't been going out that long. They didn't even spend every night together, even if she was there six nights out of seven, and had left her toothbrush there. Something she'd never done voluntarily before. She'd only admitted that she loved him on their holiday together. It was too soon. But what other question could he want to ask? And why did he reach into his pocket every time he tried to say it?

By the time she'd got to Agatha's, her legs burned from the exercise and her head swirled. She almost bumped into her sister as she threw open the gate.

"You OK?"

"What? Yeah, fine."

"You don't seem fine."

Why could her sister always read her emotions? She considered lying but her traitorous mouth beat her brain and she blurted out the truth.

"Mort…he wants to ask me something. Something serious."

Agatha clutched her hands to her chest. "Goddess! He's going to propose! I knew it. I knew it."

"What? No!"

"Has he spoken to you about it? Dropped any hints?"

"None." Unless she'd missed something. Why were people so difficult? "It's not that, OK? It's…something else."

"What else could he want to ask you?"

That was the problem, Fi couldn't think of anything else. "Just drop it."

"You're going to say yes, aren't you?"

"I said 'drop it'."

"Fi," Agatha grasped her hands, "you love him. I can tell. And he loves you. We're all really happy for you. Mort likes you just the way you are, which, you know, is not always…normal. You won't do any better."

"I don't want to do any better!"

"Good, then when he asks, say yes." Agatha wiped her hands on her jeans as if it was that simple.

"Where's Cress?"

"Mum took her home. Where did you get to anyway? Couldn't keep your hands off the hot doctor?"

"I went through a portal to the realm of the dead, had to fight through a maze and then the God of Death tasked me to find a necromancer."

"Right…well thank you for the cake, it was delicious, the bits of it we could salvage. Mum said sorry for ruining the icing."

Fi raised one eyebrow. "Mum said sorry?"

"Well, she meant to apologise…"

"Right." Fi knew her mother all too well and apologies did not easily cross her lips.

"And thanks for the birthday present," Agatha said through gritted teeth.

Fi grinned. "I knew you'd like him. I saw him and I thought, that's just what Aggy needs."

"Mmmm."

"And Mort's dad got you this."

Agatha took the small box and opened it to reveal three small brown seeds. "Oooo, what are they?"

"He said something about apples from the other world."

Agatha dropped the box and the seeds scattered across the path. Cluck Norris and the chickens rushed over with a surprising turn of speed. The greedy cockerel swallowed one before Agatha shooed them away and tucked the remaining seeds back into the box.

"You don't mean the silver apples of youth?"

Fi shrugged. "No idea. He said that if you could get them to grow, then you deserved them."

Agatha enveloped her in a hug. "Thank you, thank you, thank you. This makes up for that ugly gnome."

"Hey! I was never rude about your gifts."

"Why would you be rude about my gifts? They're perfect for you."

Fi rolled her eyes and prised herself from her sister's arms. "I'd better go. I'm glad you had a great birthday, Aggy."

"I did. Do you want to take Bea now?"

Fi's forehead creased.

"You promised to babysit so Neville and I could have an evening together. Remember?"

"Oh, yes. Yes. Of course."

"You forgot, didn't you?"

"No! Is she ready?"

"She was ready before the party. She was a bit upset that you left without her." Agatha lowered her voice as her daughter raced into the garden.

"Aunty Fi! Are you ready for a sleepover?"

"Absolutely Bumble Bea."

"Yay! Let's go." The small child yanked Fi out of the garden. She waved at her sister and headed over to her mum's house.

Chapter 13

Bea skipped down the path to her grandmother's house, pausing to wave to the grumpy donkey in the corner of the enormous garden.

"Hi Timmy!"

"It is Timaeus, as well thou knowst tiny mortal."

"Give over, Timmy, she's a kid."

"Then she should respect her elders." He turned back to grazing and Fi herded Bea up the path before the demon trapped in the donkey's body decided to bite someone. His moods ranged from grumpy to smitey and she knew how much a kick from an irate donkey hurt. She winced and rubbed her thigh at the unpleasant memory.

The house flung open its door as they approached. Fi smiled, glad the semi-sentient house was in a good mood.

"Granny!" Bea rushed up to her grandmother and hugged her legs. Nell leaned down and cuddled her back.

"Bea, what a lovely surprise."

"I said I'd babysit so Agatha could have her birthday night alone with Neville."

"And what have you got planned?"

Fi blinked before she blurted out the first thing that came into her head. "Video game night."

"Yay!" Bea started an impromptu dance around the kitchen table. Cressida dodged one of her feet, scrambled under the table and hissed from her safe spot.

"Oh cheer up, Cress."

It's Cressida and where have you been? I looked round and you were gone.

"Yeah, sorry about that." Fi bent down and reached under the table to scratch her familiar under the chin. "I sort of went through a portal to the other realm, had to fight my way through a maze and now have to find a necromancer."

What?

"It's pardon, not what." Fi grinned; it wasn't often she was able to correct her familiar.

You went to another realm without me. Hurt rang through Cressida's voice.

"Sorry. Tell you what, next time I go to another realm, I'll take you with me if I can."

That's all I ask.

"And what are you feeding my granddaughter for this games night?" Her mother glossed over the reference to a portal and another realm.

"Er...pizza."

"Junk food."

"Unless you want to make us something?"

Nell scoffed. "I have important WWWI business to attend to. I want to start planning the Tri-Village Halloween Fete."

"In June?"

"Best to be early, Fiona. Magewell finally have a new Chair and rumour is that he's determined to win best trick in show."

Fi shook her head at her mother's competitiveness. "So if you're too busy to cook, do you want me to order you a pizza?"

"Margherita, please."

Fi smiled and herded Bea up to her room. She picked up discarded clothes from the floor and shoved them into the washing basket to make some room.

If I'd have known all it took was your niece coming over for you to tidy this dump, I would have suggested it months ago.

"OK, what pizza toppings do you want?" Fi took out her phone and opened the app to place the order. She clicked on the discount that flashed up for regular customers and pushed away the wave of shame that came with the thank you message. She didn't want to be reminded how many pizzas she'd ordered this month.

"Pineapple."

"Pineapple? On pizza? Are you really my niece?"

Bea giggled. "Silly Aunty Fi."

"OK, we'll do half and half; pineapple and cheese for you, pepperoni for me. Mum wants a plain cheese. Cressida, anything for you?"

There's a steak in the fridge.

"OK, no pizza for you. And we'll have some doughballs and cookies. There. Order placed."

Bea did another dance, whacking Fi's desk and making her computer shudder.

"Careful, if that thing falls, it's game over. Literally." Fi nudged her niece over to the bed to protect her computer. It was the first one she'd built and the only piece of technology that survived any length of time around her unpredictable magic even with all the upgrades she'd done over the years.

"Your room is so cool, Aunty Fi. My posters are nothing like these."

Fi looked round at the posters and gulped. There were a lot of half-naked characters from videogames that probably weren't age appropriate. "Er, I've been meaning to redecorate."

"Cool, can I have that one when you take them down?" The girl pointed to a succubus in wisps of black cloth making a provocative pose.

"Er, not that one. How about this nice blue hedgehog?"

"Cool."

Fi took it down, grimacing as one of the blobs of blu-tack tore the wallpaper. The house gave a tiny shudder then settled down. Fi took that as tacit approval and took down a couple more while her niece studied the picture with wide eyes.

"OK, I'll cook Cressida's steak, then we can start. What do you want to play?"

Bea flounced over to the stack of game cases piled high against a wall. She picked one and waved it. "This one."

Fi grabbed the game and hugged it to her, hiding the gory bloodstains printed on the cover from her niece. "That's a bit old for you, see the eighteen in the corner. Why don't I get some you can choose from?"

Fi hastily returned the copy of Resident Evil and selected all the age-appropriate ones. She dumped them on the bed and Bea perused them as if she were making the biggest decision of her young life.

"I want to start with the cars, then this pink one."

"You got it. I'll set you up with Mario Kart and be back up in a jiffy."

With Bea safely sat racing a princess round the easiest track, Fi hurried downstairs to cook Cressida's steak – rare, the more blood oozing out the better – and collect the pizza from a young delivery man in a baggy uniform. She left her mother's order on the kitchen side and raced back upstairs. The house grumbled by shaking the steps as she climbed up.

"It's OK, I'll use napkins."

Appeased, the house allowed her upstairs where she set out a feast of junk food for both of them before jumping on the second controller and racing her niece around the Mushroom Kingdom.

Chapter 14

"Aunty Fi! Aunty Fi!"

Fiona woke to the creak of her niece bouncing on her bed. "How are you awake? It's only –" she checked her phone. "Six thirty!" Fi groaned and covered her eyes with her arm. "How? You stayed up until eleven!"

"Can I have a cookie for breakfast? Please, Aunty Fi."

"Will it keep you quiet?"

"Yep, magic club salute." The girl did an imitation of waving a magic wand and grabbed a chocolate cookie from the cardboard box. "What are we doing today?" she asked through a mouthful of crumbs.

Another one who talks with her mouth full. Cressida hopped down from her spot on the chair. *I'll be downstairs if you need me.* The golden wyrm padded over to the door and waited expectantly for it to open. The house obliged and she sauntered downstairs.

"Doing? You're going back to Aggy's, I mean, your mum's," Fi said from underneath her arm. How did the child have so much energy? It wasn't like she stayed still while she was asleep. Fi had contemplated leaving the bed to her and sleeping on the floor after the second punch to her head.

"I know, but they won't be here for hours. So, can we play more games?"

"Er, sure. After breakfast."

"I've finished my cookie."

"I'm not sure your mum will let me babysit again if she knew all you had was a cookie. Why don't we find some real food?" And coffee, she added silently. She needed caffeine if she had any hope of keeping up with her energetic niece.

Her mother was already downstairs, frying up bacon and sausages for the Bed & Breakfast guests.

"You're up early."

Fi grunted. Bea ran in circles round the table, tapping each chair as she went. Nell poured a cup of Goblin Blend coffee and passed it over to her daughter.

Fi smiled and took a sip. "Thanks. I don't know how you did it."

"Did what?"

"Raised two kids. We were never like that, were we?"

Her mother snorted. "You were worse, always running about, knocking something over. And at least with Bea I don't have to worry about fires."

"That was one time!"

"You nearly burned down the house."

"It has sprinklers."

"Only since you hit puberty."

Fi's brow creased as she thought back. Maybe her mum was right, she didn't remember sprinklers before she went to secondary school, but it wasn't exactly the type of thing a child would notice.

"So, what are your plans for the morning?"

"Er…videogames."

"Yay!" Bea twirled around her grandmother and aunt before sitting at the table. Nell placed a bowl of sugary cereal in front of her.

"How come you never let us have sugar at breakfast?"

"Because I'm your mother, I have to look after your health."

"But Bea's your granddaughter."

"Precisely. I get to spoil her. She's my reward for not killing you and your sister."

Fi laughed. At least, she thought it was a joke.

After breakfast, she cajoled Bea into getting dressed with promises of more games and they raced and beat each other up on screen until Agatha arrived.

She peeked through the door. "Coo-eee. Mummy's here, darling."

"Hi Mum. Can I stay with Aunty Fi today?"

"I don't think that's a good idea. Granny's already told me about your late night yesterday." She gave Fi a pointed look.

"Why don't you get your things and meet me downstairs? Nice to see you tidied up for your niece, Fi."

"I did…" Fi trailed off. The empty pizza boxes didn't help her case. Agatha nodded like she'd won something and headed downstairs. Fi gathered up the rubbish and followed her.

"How's Gnomeo getting along?"

"Good." Agatha's voice was tight. She clearly wanted Fi to drop any references to the ugly garden ornament.

Fi smirked. "I bet he's fitting right in at gnome."

Agatha smiled, unable to resist a pun exchange with her sister. "Gnome, sweet gnome."

"Go big or go gnome."

"Gnome on the range."

"Gnome on the patio more like."

"Oh gnome you didn't. That was rubbish!" Agatha was right. Her sister won that round of puns.

"What are you two jabbering on about?" their mother asked.

"Nothing," they answered in unison.

Nell looked between them. "Sometimes, it's like you live in your own world."

"Gnome world," they said together before bursting into giggles.

Fi's phone blared out the Imperial Death March. "Hello."

"Fiona? It's Detective Ledd. I'm at the coroner's office. I think you should come over."

"Decided I'm not a suspect?" Fi couldn't keep the sarcasm from her voice. She had been one hundred per cent sure she hadn't done it.

"You're not a suspect anymore. He was already dead."

Chapter 15

"What?"

"Can you get here?"

"Give me a minute – Aggy, can I borrow the car?"

"Sorry, it's in the garage, and you're not insured."

Fi swore. Looks like she was going to have to fly. "I'll be there. About forty minutes, as the vacuum flies."

She hung up, grabbed a jacket and her trusty X-5000 cyclone vacuum cleaner and laced up her converse trainers. "Fancy a ride, Cressida?"

After all that racket last night and the early start this morning, I think I'll stay here and catch up on my sleep, thank you.

"Suit yourself."

Wait!

"You want to come?"

No. Can you take a picture of me by the fire. For my followers.

"Unbelievable."

And can you check the comments?

"You know I'm on a case, going to the morgue."

Cressida gave her a look. If the wyrm could have raised an eyebrow, she would have.

"Fine." Fi scrolled through the feed, ignoring the trolls asking for private pictures. "Everyone loves you. Someone asked if you have scale rot…"

What?! Let me see.

"Just kidding. See you later." Fi headed outside, allowed a small amount of magic to trickle into the vacuum cleaner and turned it on. It whirred and she kicked off before it had a chance to hoover up too many petals from the lawn.

Once airborne, she followed her phone's directions, cutting off corners by flying over fields. There was only one close call with a dopey pigeon before the coroner's office came into sight. She decelerated and landed on the gravel drive, her vacuum cleaner clattering as it sucked up the small pebbles before she turned it off.

Fi hurried inside, gave the X-5000 to the receptionist who accepted it with a roll of her eyes, used to the strange witch's visits, and headed to autopsy room one. She barged through the door and came face to face with a huge pair of eyes.

She screamed. He screamed, took a step back, tripped and fell onto the body laid out on the slab.

"Who are you?"

"Suresh. Who are you?" he asked, tipping up the magnifying lenses over his face.

"Fi. Where's Robbie?"

"Fiona Blair. I might have known it was you causing all that commotion."

Fi turned, her cheeks flushing as she met Detective Ledd's superior gaze. Behind him, the usual coroner grinned.

"I see you've met my new assistant. Suresh, get cleaned up and put the kettle on. We'll be through in a minute. Come on, then." Robbie strode back to the adjacent autopsy room and held the door open.

Fi slunk through; the hospital scent of cleaning fluid underpinned by the staleness of rotting flesh making her gag. She still wasn't used to that smell. She took a spot near a metal cabinet and folded her arms. "What's going on? Ledd said he was dead already."

"He was," the coroner nodded, "according to my tests, he'd been dead for forty-eight hours by the time you encountered him. See here, decomposition of internal organs is starting to set in and the skin has shrunk away from the finger nails."

"But he was walking about. Don't dead people get rigor mortis?"

"They do, but only for the first 12-24 hours, after that the muscles relax again into secondary flaccidity. That's where he is."

"But he was walking." Fi couldn't ignore that fact. "I saw him."

"That's the intriguing part."

"How did he die?"

"Cardiac arrest. Looks natural but possibly induced, I've sent off for a tox screen but it's been so long that any drugs might not be traceable. My best guess is someone animated the corpse."

"That's where you come in," said the detective.

"Me? I didn't bring anyone back to life."

"No." He rolled his eyes. "Magic."

"Necromancy," Fi breathed.

"Yes."

The God of Death had been right. There was a necromancer operating in the Cotswolds.

"I think I need a coffee."

"Excellent, well I think Suresh should be done by now. Let's see if he can make a decent cuppa." Robbie led the way to the small kitchenette at the back of the building and Fi slumped into one of the outdated orange chairs.

"So, what are you going to do about this necromancer?" The detective got straight to the point. Normally, Fi would have appreciated his direct approach, but today, when she had no idea how to track down a magical being who could raise the dead, it was irritating.

"I've got people looking into it."

"Already?" The detective frowned. "But we've only just told you about it."

"Someone mentioned it yesterday."

"Who?"

"The God of Death."

"If you can't be serious, Fiona, I don't know how we can work together on this."

"OK, it doesn't matter who told me. Say it's an informant. I've got someone looking into it." She rubbed her eyes. "But where did they get Mr Kite's body?"

The coroner shrugged, nearly spilling her cup of tea. "I looked up the death certificate. Nothing."

"So it's someone in the system? Maybe at the hospital."

"Or someone killed him."

Fi stared at the detective. That was the worst possible option. Necromancy was bad enough, but a killer as well.

"Sorry, can you repeat that?" In her worries about necromancy, she'd missed the last part of the conversation.

"I said, 'can you trace a magical signature or something like that?'"

"I wish. I mean, it's possible, I suppose, but it's not very precise. Like, I could sense magic on Mr Kite, but I couldn't even tell what sort of magic it was, it just felt…cold." Like death, she thought. So that was necromantic magic. Fi shivered.

"Is there anyone else who can help? Maybe your coven?"

"I don't have a coven and that's an old-fashioned idea anyway. Only teenagers trying to be cool have covens nowadays." The detective flinched at her words and Fi frowned as she carried on. "I'll ask my mum, see if she knows anything. If any of the WWWI members are acting weird, she'd be the first to know."

"I'll let you know if the tox results come back with anything," said Robbie, taking a long drink of her tea.

Detective Ledd stood. "Great. Fi, I'll walk you out."

Fi walked alongside the detective in awkward silence until he coughed. "So, Fi, that thing you said about the coven…"

"It's fine, you didn't know. It's not something we witches really care about." She didn't care anyway and which other witches was the detective going to speak to?

"No, I mean," he shuffled his feet, "are there any other words I should avoid when talking to…magical beings." Fi narrowed her eyes and he floundered. "Is that an offensive term?"

"Why are you so interested in not offending magical beings? I thought you didn't like supernaturals…"

He coughed again and avoided eye contact. "I just thought I should change, evolve, you know." She cocked an eyebrow, a small smile brewing on her lips and stayed silent, enjoying him squirm. "If you must know, I've started seeing someone. A warlock. There. Now you know."

"A warlock? Is she…he local?"

"She is from London, I met her on a dating app."

"What's her name?"

"I'm not telling you. You'll look her up."

"Well not everyone on a dating app is who they say they are."

"Miranda is!"

"Miranda?"

"We met up in London last weekend and I realised that I don't know a lot about the supernatural world and I don't want to offend her by saying something stupid."

"Larry, I'm impressed." This was genuine growth from the detective.

"So, is there anything I shouldn't say? You know, to your kind."

Not that much growth then.

"Just don't use any of the insulting words for supernaturals and you'll be fine. Honest." She saw the pleading look in his eyes. "If I think of anything, I'll let you know."

She patted him on the shoulder and retrieved her vacuum cleaner from the receptionist, eyeing the downpour outside. "I don't suppose you're heading to Omensford…"

"Come on, I'll give you a lift."

Chapter 16

Agatha glared out of her window at the offensive gnome that messed up her garden aesthetic. "Did you move the gnome, Neville?"

"Hmmm? Gnome? In the garden."

Agatha sighed. She should have known better than to interrupt his miniature painting.

"Bea, darling, did you move mummy's gnome?"

"Nope." Her daughter's tongue crept out as she concentrated on her maths homework.

Agatha frowned. Someone had moved the ghastly thing. It was no longer by her antique bird bath – rescued from going to landfill thanks to a tip off from one of the WWWI – and now stood by the outside tap. The gaudy colours looked more faded as well, but maybe that was her imagination. She picked at a bit of dirt under her fingernail. There was only one person she knew immature enough to try to wind her up by moving a garden gnome.

"Neville, I'm going out. Make sure Bea's got enough clothes for school."

She marched over to her mother's house, straight through the gate, ignoring the demon donkey who snored in a corner of the garden, and down the path until she got to the door. It refused to open.

"Oh, come on. I'm not going to hurt anyone. I just need to talk to my sister."

The door didn't budge.

"I promise I won't hurt anyone." She did a mock salute. It seemed to impress the semi-sentient house enough because the door opened slowly. Agatha slipped inside before it could change its mind.

"Fiona!" she bellowed.

"I'm here, you don't have to shout." Fi rubbed her ears.

"Right," Agatha took a breath to compose herself. She'd wanted to raise her voice, but she could hardly do that when her sister was inconsiderately right in front of her in the kitchen. "What have you done to the gnome?"

"The gnome?"

"Don't play dumb with me. The gnome that you bought me."

"He has a name."

"Stop messing with him."

"What?" Fiona looked confused, but Agatha wasn't fooled.

"You moved him."

"I didn't!"

"Just stop it."

"I'm not lying. Why would I move your gnome? Hang on, does this mean you've taken him out from under the bird bath?"

"No–"

"I cannot believe you would try to hide the gift I got you. I searched everywhere for the perfect gnome, and you're here accusing me of – what are you accusing me of?"

"You came into my garden and moved it. I don't know what games you're playing, but it's not funny."

"Aggy, I swear to you that I haven't touched your gnome since I put him in your garden at your birthday party."

"Really?" Agatha sank into a chair, her anger deflating like the leftover birthday balloons that still littered her house.

"Of course not, why would I do that?"

"To wind me up."

"Well, maybe, if I'd thought of it. But I've been busy with this case and – no, Aggy, I haven't been in your garden."

"Then who's touched my gnome?"

Fi shrugged and offered her sister a cup of tea before turning back to her baking. It was so unfair that her sister could bake like a goddess while staying as thin as a vine. Agatha sank into a kitchen chair.

"It's just so…odd. So, how are things with you?"

"Well there's this weird case at work–"

"I meant, you and Mort."

"Oh."

"Has he popped the question?"

"No, and he's not going to."

"How do you know?"

"There haven't been any signs."

Agatha raised her eyebrows. "Signs? Like him wanting to ask you a question and getting nervous? *That sort of sign?*"

"No, like…hints. No one would just ask someone to marry them without hints. And we haven't had any of the marriage conversations."

"Marriage conversations?"

"Yeah, like about kids and stuff."

Agatha took a sip of her tea.

"How did Neville propose?"

"It was lovely. We were on holiday together up in Scotland, and the weather was awful, so we were at home in this cabin with the log burner going, but he managed to get this big bunch of roses for me and set it up in the hall so I found it when I came in from collecting wood. Then there was this trail of petals to our bedroom, and there he was, down on one knee in the middle of more petals holding out this beautiful ring." Agatha spun the gold band on her finger, a misty smile playing on her lips as she remembered the most romantic thing her husband had done for her. "He said he'd done the sums and me plus him equalled happiness forever. And he chose the inlaid diamonds so they wouldn't catch when I worked in the garden. Then we had champagne – the real stuff, not prosecco – and then I called Mum and told her just before the house hung up on me. Do you remember how much it sulked because he didn't do it here? I couldn't come round for weeks. And after that, he laid me down in front of the fire and–"

"Do not finish that sentence." Fi gagged.

Agatha smirked. "Let's just say it was the best night of my life."

Her sister made a puking sound before she spoke. "But, see. It was romantic, planned, not something that he just asked you. He's not going to propose."

"If you say so."

"He's not!"

"You know him best." Agatha smiled at Fiona's glare. They were both adults now, but it was still too easy to wind up her little sister.

Although, she had no idea why Fi was so worked up about this. A proposal was a good thing, the perfect way to cement her relationship with Mort and finally bring her sister into adulthood. Anyone could see how much they cared for each other, and it was so rare to form that sort of understanding with another human. She'd been lucky with Neville, her handsome accountant, and she just wanted her baby sister to be happy too.

"Fiona, Agatha, my favourite daughters." Both women eyed their mother with suspicion. "There's no need to look at me like that, can't a mother greet her daughters?"

"I suppose."

"I was just wondering whether either of you were free on Wednesday."

"I'd have to check the calendar," Agatha said, careful not to admit that she had no plans on Wednesday.

"I've got a case," Fi said.

"I need someone to come and talk to the WWWI, our speaker has let us down."

"Sorry, Mum, I've got a case," Fi repeated.

"Hmmm, yes, I know. I think it'd be perfect for you to come and reassure our members that you're doing all you can to keep our community safe. I'll pencil you in."

Agatha patted Fi's hand in silent commiseration and support as her sister's mouth opened and closed wordlessly. The last time Agatha had agreed to be the guest speaker for one of the Witches', Wizards' and Warlocks' Institute meetings, she'd found herself giving a guided tour of the village pointing out plants of interest.

"I'd better go," Agatha said, downing the last of her tea.

"Are you sure? I think I need to do some more stress baking. How do you feel about brownies?"

"Tempting, but we've still got a lot of cake left from the party." Agatha patted her stomach. "And it's not helping my diet."

"Diets! Really, you don't need to diet." That was easy for her mother to say; the older woman was stick thin and her sister had inherited her genes, but Agatha had a fondness for cakes and sweets that overrode the time she spent doing physical exercise in the garden.

Agatha bit down on any response to her mother, it would only fall on deaf ears or worse end with some sort of regimented plan. "See you later." She rushed out of the house and speed walked home, maybe if she moved her legs faster, it would offset the massive slice of cake she was about to have.

She dodged the cockerel as she entered the garden and shooed him round the back with practiced motions. Her shoulders relaxed as she surveyed her flowerbeds and the vegetable patch, and all her tension fell away. This was her haven, her sanctuary and that made whatever was going on with the gnome even worse.

Agatha bent down and plucked a weed from the dark soil with vengeance, before checking the underside of the bean leaves for any signs of pests, while she was down there. Satisfied, she stood and went in.

As she washed her hands in the stainless-steel sink, she caught sight of the mound of washing still next to the machine.

"Neville?"

Her husband looked up from the sea of miniature models in front of him, the magnifying goggles over his eyes making him look like a strange insect. "Yes, dear."

"Why aren't Bea's clothes washed?"

"You said she has enough clothes."

"I said 'make sure she has enough school clothes'."

"Ah."

"What have you done while I've been out?" she asked with some trepidation, noting the army laid out in front of her husband and the paint pots lined up in a neat row next to Bea's maths homework.

"Well, I thought the army could use a spruce." He held up a model. It was a spiderlike creature the size of her thumb and now sported a tiny top hat and neatly painted moustache. "I'm calling them the Warhatters. What do you think?"

"I think I need to do the washing because you've spent over two hours gluing top hats to plastic aliens."

Chapter 17

Fi put down the empty cake tin with a satisfying clunk before making a coffee and sinking into a chair. Steve had been happy with her stress baking efforts and welcomed the brownies with gusto, and now she could put her feet up and relax and try to pretend that there wasn't a necromancer running around the Cotswolds and her boyfriend didn't want to propose to her. Just for five minutes.

"Knock, knock." Mort entered and Fi jumped up from her seat.

"Mort! What are you doing here?"

"I thought we could work on the case together. I sent a text."

Fi checked her phone. The text alert stared back at her. Stupid silent setting

"Why don't you take him to your room, Fiona?" Her mother looked up from her colour coded binder.

"Er, I could bring the laptop downstairs, there's more space."

"Nonsense. I need some peace to plan our WWWI agendas. Tell me, doctor, would you be interested in speaking to us about first aid or home remedies for common illnesses?"

"I suppose."

"Excellent, that's our September speaker slot filled." Nell wrote Mort's name in her planner with a flourish.

"Come on, let's get upstairs before she nobbles you for any more meetings."

"I heard that," Nell said without looking up.

Fi trudged upstairs and nudged her bedroom door open. She let out a sigh of relief. It was still mostly tidy from her niece's sleepover, and she only had to pick up two items of discarded clothing.

Mort stood in the doorway, surveying the room. "Nice posters."

Cressida tsked in her mind.

Fi's cheeks flushed. "They're characters. From videogames."

"I can see."

"I just haven't got round to redecorating since I moved back in…" she trailed off. She'd been back at her mum's for over a year, it was about time she redecorated or moved out. She had enough savings now, but it didn't feel right to leave her mum on her own with a bad leg, and the couple renting out her cottage were lovely and covered her mortgage payments. She couldn't kick them out.

Mort smiled. "Hey, it's better than my teenage room. I had anatomical charts up on my wall."

"Really?"

He shrugged. "I had to study to get the grades to go to medical school."

"Even though you didn't want to be a doctor?"

He shuffled his feet. "It wasn't that simple. I thought I had to be a doctor to make Mum and Dad proud, and they were fighting a lot – it was just before the divorce – and it was easier to focus on my studies and escape into books and medical journals."

"So you really didn't have anything else on your wall?"

"Well, there was this one print of a skull – it was from a heavy metal band and I thought it was so cool, because of our connection with Arawn."

"Did you even listen to their music?"

"Yes! I even went to a gig."

"Mr rock and roll."

He laughed.

"Want to help me take them down?"

"I think I'd rather make out like we were teenagers…"

Cressida made a hacking sound. *I think that's my cue to leave.*

"Cressida – what's got into you?"

Her familiar didn't deign to reply and stalked off with her tail held straight.

"Sorry about her."

"No worries. We should probably talk about the case anyway – business first, then pleasure."

"OK," Fi cleared her chair of the clothes she'd deposited there and plonked herself down in front of her trusty computer – the one piece of tech that had lasted through her power surges and temperamental teenage years. With a couple of clicks, she loaded up a new report and typed as she spoke. "You know that guy I had to deal with before the party."

"The one causing a traffic jam on the High Street?"

"That's him. Mr Kite. Well…he was dead."

"That's awful, and you saw him so recently."

"No. He was dead. When I found him. Walking about."

"Wow."

"Yep. So Arawn was right – there's a necromancer about."

"Do you know anything else?"

She shook her head. "He died of a heart attack. Coroner's checking for drugs, but nothing unusual so far. Except for him still moving. What about you?"

"Dad found this in our library." Mort placed a small leatherbound book on her desk and opened it to a bookmarked page. He coughed and read aloud, "Necromancers are powerful magic users who seek mastery over life through death. One such being had plagued the moors of Devonshire for almost a year before I was notified through the newly found Bureau of Magical Affairs."

"Goes on a bit, doesn't he?"

"It's a diary from the seventeenth century. Shall I carry on?"

Fi nodded and turned back to her screen, her fingers blurring over the keyboard as she captured the essence of the long-winded tale.

"It was a dark night in November when, with the aid of Miss Smythe – the delectable Dorothea – I finally caught up with the beast in a lonely crypt where he had made his lair. After smiting two of his apparitions, I entered the stone grave and a chill crept down my spine as I spied him across the cold room.

"He was of middling height, with nothing in his outward appearance to suggest he conspired with such dark arts save his sallow complexion, which spoke of time away from the sun. Dorothea suggested we run him through, but compassion and, I must confess, a desire to learn more of his motives, stilled my hand. Instead, I conversed with the creature, with an aim to win his trust and perhaps study him more closely at the Bureau.

"He was unphased by my questions and, indeed, regarded himself as a scholar rather than a creature of darkness. The man – Nimbleby, was his name – answered my questions amiably and regretted that he had no refreshments to offer us, but his tea had run out the day before and he had no nourishment save the rats that he caught in this dank place.

"Dorothea made a most unladylike sound at that, and I paused to affirm that her vampiric instincts were in check. That being done, I inquired as to why Nimbleby had committed such a heinous crime against nature as to raise the dead.

"He replied that he had found a book that said it was possible and he had explored that possibility to its fullest, starting with small animals and working up to the poor creatures we had dispatched in the graveyard. He was eager to share his theories and my stomach sickened as he listed the experiments he had undertaken to determine the best route to success.

"It transpired that the fresher the corpse, the easier it was to raise from its natural state and the longer it would last, but he confessed that he was unable to always control the puppets as it required considerable will for them to perform the simplest task.

"Again, I asked him why, not quite knowing why I prolonged the conversation, except that a macabre fascination had come over me and I found I could not stop.

"Perhaps sensing a kindred spirit, the necromancer held up a miniature of a woman with a fair complexion and a simple look of kindness upon her painted face. He confessed to me that she was his love, and they were affianced until death claimed her the week before their marriage. He sought to forget his sorrows through travel, and it was on the continent where he found this knowledge and studied it, until he had some small success with dogs and other small mammals.

"It was only then that he returned to England to refine his studies and be closer to his fiancée when he judged the time right. I confess that this knowledge struck my heart as surely as any blade, for who knows the dark pain of grief more surely than I?

"But he must have sensed my weakness, for he conjured a spell of murky shadow that seemed set upon drawing my very essence from my body. With a curse, I groped for my pistol, but I was too slow.

"It was Dorothea who struck the blow, her inhuman speed far superior to my own. When she turned to me after, her eyes glowed red and she told me in simple terms that I was a fool consumed by knowledge. Perhaps she was right. She made to take the book and destroy it, but I stilled her hand and took this arcane knowledge into my custody. I had every intention of handing it into the Bureau, but, instead, I have it here on my desk.

"It calls to me. It is mere paper and ink, of that I am sure, but it tempts me so…for if I could uncover its secrets and master its contents, I could surely raise my dear Cordelia and speak with her once more. But I know I cannot yield, for it is too dangerous and too easy, even for one with a god's protection, to fall to darkness."

Fi let out a low whistle. "He sounds mad. What did he do with the book?"

Mort flipped forward a few pages and squinted at the small print. "I write this passage with shaking hands. I do not know what possessed me, but tonight, on the anniversary of Cordelia's passing, I opened the book. The words surrounded me, and the temptation was great. I spoke the first few as if something else drove my mouth, before I got hold of my senses and closed the tome.

"I, who am able to pass to the other realm and speak with my love, want still to see her in flesh and blood again. To see her whole and touch her creamy skin and press my lips to hers. It is a temptation that I cannot shake. And I feel the call of the damned book still, from where I have thrown it on the floor. I should never have taken it. One thing is clear. I must destroy this book, the knowledge is too great."

Fi and Mort exchanged a look.

"And did he, destroy it?"

Mort turned the pages. "In a later entry, he says he couldn't bring himself to destroy it, so he hid it, and I quote, 'I dare not reveal the location, even to entrust it to the pages of this diary, lest others be tempted as I was'."

Fi swivelled in her office chair. "So…someone found the book and is using it."

"It's a theory."

"OK…" Fi drummed her fingers on her desk as she thought. "So, we don't know where the book was hidden or who found it. But maybe we can find out more about necromancy. Come with me."

Chapter 18

Fi led Mort downstairs, away from the embarrassment of her bedroom, and to the library. It was a dark room in the centre of the house and the books rustled on their shelves as they entered. A large book flew across the room. Mort ducked to avoid being hit on the head by the spine.

"Wow. This is…different to our library." Mort turned slowly, taking in the floor to ceiling shelves lined with books. He reached for a book and the volume shrank back deeper into the shelves, disappearing behind other books. "What the –?"

"Don't try to work it out, the dimensions of the library are one of the great mysteries. I think it's somehow linked to every magical library around the world – I'm sure I saw Egyptian Hieroglyphs down here once – but I don't know how it works." Fi coughed. "House, this is Mortimer De'ath. He's a…friend of mine, a good friend, boyfriend."

She paused and took a breath, ignoring the twitch of Mort's lips at her rambling. When she felt back in control, she carried on, "And he's helping me with some research."

Fi waited, not sure how the magical house would react to a stranger in one of its most important rooms.

The pages settled down to their usual whispering and the flying book floated back to its position on the shelves.

"We need to know anything you've got on necromancy."

The shuffling pages redoubled in volume and the room shook. Fi grabbed onto Mort as the library started to launch books at them. Fi flattened herself onto the carpet, pulling Mort down with her. "I was afraid of this."

Nell burst into the library. "Necromancy?!"

Fi jumped up from the floor. "It's about the case I'm working on." Books circled her.

Her mother looked her up and down and sniffed. "Alright then." She turned to the shelves and ran one long finger over the nearest one, soothing the house. "It's alright, do as she asks."

With a judgemental shudder, the room stopped shaking and the flying books returned to their places. There was a long, drawn out pause as the house drew on whatever magic powered the library. Then several books and scrolls slid out from their positions. Fi walked round the room, gathering up the volumes before laying them on the low coffee table. The house let out another tremor when she dropped one on the floor.

"Sorry, sorry. I'll be more careful. You know, it would be a lot easier to do my job if the house trusted me instead of telling tales any time I try to use the library."

Fi's mum tutted. "You can't blame the house. It's protective and quite keen to avoid people finding out about the more dangerous branches of magic. Besides, your track record isn't great."

"I was fifteen!"

"Old enough to know better. Honestly."

"I only wanted to know what they looked like."

"But demons, Fiona."

"It was for a videogame…" Fi trailed off. It had been a stupid decision to try to research demons, but she'd wanted to prove that the 8-bit versions weren't anything like the real thing. She shook her head. What they needed now was something on necromancy. "OK, I'm sorry. I haven't told you this, house, but I work for the Magical Liaison Office and I sometimes need to look up bad things. OK, all happy now?"

The fire crackled in the marble fireplace and the house gave a sigh.

"Great. Now, let's get started. Mort, grab a book."

Fi watched Mort's face pale as he selected a large tome bound with brown leather. "Is that a tattoo?"

"Er, maybe. Some of these books are quite old and…"

"It's bound with human skin, dear. You're a doctor, aren't you? Stop being so squeamish." Nell took the book from him and handed him a more traditionally bound volume.

Fi gave him a sympathetic smile and picked up one of the scrolls. The words chased themselves around the page before settling into English and allowing her to read them. She scanned the text; dire warnings, one of the worst branches of blood magic, terrible things happen if spells go wrong, blah, blah, blah.

Her eyes stopped on a picture of a wizard coated in red. She blinked. Nope. Not coated in blood, he'd been turned inside out by a necromantic spell gone wrong. She forced down the bile that gathered in the back of her throat and pushed the scroll away, reaching for a more modern book.

An hour later, Fi rubbed her eyes in an attempt to chase away the disturbing images she'd seen. "This is useless. Lots of warnings and tales of necromancy gone wrong but nothing concrete."

Nell sniffed. "What were you expecting, dear? The Ladybird guide to necromancy?"

"No, but, I wanted more than vague hints about the Book of Souls."

"At least now we know that's what it's called," Mort said.

Fi shot Mort a smile. He was always the optimist. She stretched. "But we don't know anything else."

Nell checked the time and stood, smoothing down her ankle-length skirt. "I'm going to start dinner. Warn me if you plan to ask the house about any other dark magic." She swept out of the room.

Fi huffed a sigh and pulled another book towards her, scanning the pages for anything useful. Nothing. Not even a spell to contain a necromancer. "I don't think there's anything here…so our best bet is to follow Mr Kite's last steps and see who he came into contact with."

"Sounds like a plan…"

"But?"

"But, it's dinnertime."

Fi's stomach rumbled and she pressed her hands into her midriff, embarrassed at her body's sudden noise. "I guess it is."

"Can I take you out somewhere?"

"It's family night, Agatha and her lot are coming over."

Mort's face fell.

Fi covered his hand with hers. "I didn't say no."

Her mother stood by the large range cooker, adding spices to one of three large pans with one hand, while checking the WWWI planner with the other all while speaking into a phone headset tucked under her chin. Her walking stick lay abandoned against the kitchen counter.

"I'm sure he'd love to come…yes I can clear it with the palace secretary…what do you mean he doesn't do local engagements? We're in England. He should support his subjects."

"Is your mum on the phone to the King?"

Fi groaned. Her mother glanced over her shoulder. "Fi, would you stir that pot?"

"Sorry, Mum, no can do. I'm going out. With Mort."

"On family night?"

"Last minute thing. About the case."

"I see." Nell's voice was flat, and she raised an eyebrow.

"Good night, Mrs Blair."

"Good night both of you. Should I expect you back tonight, Fiona?"

Fi blushed. "Er…"

"I'll take that as a no. Well don't let me hold you up, but you might have said something, now we'll have leftovers for days."

"Sorry, Mum." Fi tugged Mort out of the door and let out a sigh of relief as soon as they were in the garden. "Sorry about that."

"We can stay for dinner, if you want."

"I really don't want."

"OK, where to? Sorella's."

It was tempting but Fi shook her head. "I had pizza last night. How about a curry?"

"I know just the place."

Chapter 19

Mort drove them to The Maharajah in Magewell. It was his favourite curry house and had the benefit of not being in Omensford, which meant that they were less likely to see anyone they knew. The owner greeted them with a smile and ushered them to a table at the back of the busy restaurant.

Fi ordered a half Indian lager and lime and Mort asked for a pint of the same beer as they perused the menu. Fi studied all the choices before selecting her standard order; the delicately spiced biryani. Mort went for a lamb balti and they agreed to share a pilau rice, a naan, and onion bhajis.

"The Bombay aloo is very good," said the server with a practiced attempt at upselling.

"We'll take it, and two poppadoms, please," Mort ordered with a smile.

The young server nodded and bowed himself away to give the order to the kitchen. Mort raised his glass and Fi chinked hers with his.

"Cheers."

Mort unfolded and refolded his napkin twice before he coughed. "I was going to wait until after we'd eaten, but there's something I wanted to ask you."

Fi swallowed her drink and clenched her fists as her entire body tightened with tension. Why did people always want to change a good thing? She was comfortable in this relationship, the first time she'd felt at ease with almost anyone else, and instead of enjoying it, she was afraid of her boyfriend asking a simple question. But…marriage?

It was a big commitment. Would he want her to take his name? Fiona De'ath. She swallowed again, unsure about the sound of it ringing around her head. Where would they live? It was all too soon.

They'd only been on one holiday together, and she wasn't sure it even counted as a holiday when they'd spent most of the time tracking down the piskie queen. She tried to focus on Mort's mouth, but her ears filled with the sound of a kettle boiling. It was too hot. She took another drink. Why was it so hot in here?

A commotion near the window jerked Fi out of her spiralling thoughts. Someone bumped into the glass and the couple nearest the window screamed in shock. Outside, a large man stood, staring at the restaurant. He tried to enter again through the window, and after a couple of false starts, found the door and shuffled inside to nervous laughter from the tables nearest the entrance. He made his way to the bar where he collapsed onto a stool.

"Can I help you, sir?" The young man behind the polished counter asked, eyeing the customer.

The man gave a gargling gurgle and the waiter swallowed.

"I didn't understand that, sir. What can I get for you, please?"

Another gargle, as if his vocal cords couldn't sound out the words. Fi stared at the newcomer. His skin was grey, and his eyes glazed white. She kicked Mort under the table and motioned with her head. He turned to follow her gaze.

"You think…?"

"Not sure. Let me try something." Fi reached out with her magic and her stomach sank.

All around her, the restaurant sparked with electrical activity, from the overhead lighting to the flashing neurons of the patrons. Fi screwed up her face against the sensory overload and concentrated on the man by the bar. Nothing. No spark, just a strange, cold sensation of magic that froze her spine.

She stood, pushing her chair back so hard that it bumped into the table behind her. Fi nodded to her boyfriend and made her way across the restaurant, glad of Mort's comforting solid presence behind her.

Fi put a hand on the man's shoulder, his skin cold through the thin shirt he wore. He turned and stared blankly at her. Mort checked his pulse, met her eyes, and shook his head.

"Come on, let's go."

"Is there a problem, madam?" The barman blinked at her, his brown eyes wide and innocent.

She flashed her ID. "Just a routine magical occurrence, nothing to worry about. I'll just take Mr...this man home. Come on, sir, let's go."

The man was a dead weight and Mort stepped up to grab his other arm. The man dragged his feet as they manoeuvred him outside. He stopped moving when they were ten paces from the restaurant. Fi staggered forward under the full weight of his body.

"What the–?"

Mort heaved and they laid him down on the cold, hard pavement on the Magewell High Street. A movement in the corner of her eye made Fi turn her head. A dark figure ran away from the High Street. She stood and chased after it, but by the time she got to the end of the street, they had vanished, and Fi had a stitch. She rubbed her side, fumbled her phone out of her pocket and called the emergency services, then she rang Detective Ledd.

"What?" he gasped down the phone.

"Are you alright? You sound out of breath," Fi said.

"On a run. Why are you calling?"

"There's another zombie, well, it was a zombie, now it's just a body."

"On my way."

The waiter ran out into the street carrying a brown paper bag. He stopped dead as he saw them crouched over a body. "I brought your curry."

Blue lights flashed over the road, making him seem younger than he was. Fi took the proffered bag, put her arm round his shoulder and led him back inside. There were some things that people shouldn't have to deal with, and zombies were top of that list.

Chapter 20

Fi supervised the body into the ambulance and answered the police's questions for the next hour, before Detective Ledd showed up, still in his sweaty jogging bottoms and ill-fitting top.

"What took you so long?"

"I had to jog back home first, then I came straight here. And this bloody watch is going off every five seconds."

"Oh." Fi remembered the modification she'd made to the settings. She took in the beads of sweat dripping down the detective's podgy face and his quivering moustache. "Let me have a look." She tapped at the screen until it was back to normal then she muted the alarm for inactivity.

"So, what happened here, then?"

Fi repeated herself until he was satisfied.

"And how were you involved?"

"What?"

"You found the first stiff, and now this one. Are you some sort of zombie magnet?"

"No! I was called to a disturbance because Mr Kite was blocking traffic – you called me, remember? – and we were just getting a curry when the corpse walked in."

"Why would a dead body want a curry?"

"No idea. I'll add it to my list of questions, along with who is the necromancer and why are they bringing people back in the first place."

"Alright. No need to be tetchy."

Fi kept her mouth shut. There was every need to be tetchy. There was a necromancer on the loose, bodies turning up during dinner and her boyfriend was possibly about to propose at any minute. And she hadn't eaten. She rubbed her stomach to ease the gnawing emptiness inside her.

"So, no leads then?"

Fi shook her head. "But when I find something, you'll be the first to know."

Behind the detective, a black portal swirled into being at the end of the street until it was a shimmering oval disk that captured a night sky not found on this plane of existence.

"Got to go. I'll let you know when I find anything." She grabbed Mort and jerked her head towards the portal. "Is that what I think it is?" she whispered out of the corner of her mouth.

He sighed. "We'd better go see what he wants. It'll only be worse if he comes into this realm."

"Can't they see it?"

"Humans often only see what they expect to see. And it's dark. Who would believe there was a portal to another realm in a Cotswolds village? Come on."

Fi sent a silent apology to Cressida, as if the small wyrm could hear her. It looked like she was going to the other realm without her familiar. Again.

Mort linked his arm through hers and they walked together through the portal, which winked out behind them. Fi only had to take three deep breaths to settle her stomach this time, her body already adjusting to the supernatural method of travelling. When she opened her eyes, they were in front of an enormous palace that looked like a cross between a fairy-tale castle and a defensible stronghold.

A pack of red-eared hounds raced across the courtyard and swarmed around them before a whistle called them off.

MORTIMER GREGORIUS DE'ATH AND FIONA JOULES BLAIR. DO YOU KNOW WHY I HAVE SUMMONED YOU? A tall figure stood in front of them, his head was the same as the ram's skull only more proportionate to his body.

"You missed us?"

The god turned his glowing, green eyes to Fi and she shrank back. Sarcasm was not a good idea when speaking to a being who could kill you with a thought. Not that he would. Probably. Maybe. She hung her head.

YOU HAVE NOT YET APPREHENDED THE NECROMANCER.

Mort bowed. "Forgive us, lord. But we are closer. We now know they operate in two towns in the Cotswolds."

YOU MUST STOP THIS ABOMINATION.

"We know."

"We're working on it," Fi added.

THE LONGER IT CONTINUES, THE MORE DANGEROUS THE SITUATION BECOMES.

"I mean, the zombies haven't exactly eaten anyone, but yeah, we know."

YOU DO NOT UNDERSTAND. WITH THEIR BODIES NOT AT REST, SOULS BECOME UNSETTLED AND THE BARRIERS BETWEEN WORLDS STRETCH THIN.

Fi looked to Mort. Her boyfriend's eyes narrowed. "Has anything breached the barrier?"

NOT YET. BUT IT IS ONLY A MATTER OF TIME. THERE ARE FORCES THAT WISH TO AID THE NECROMANCER. YOU MUST STOP THE MAGIC USER BEFORE THESE FORCES FIND THEM.

"We will." Mort bowed his head.

"Don't you have a connection with the necromancer?" Fi asked. "They're using magic to raise the dead and you're God of Death."

I HAVE A CONNECTION WITH ALL THINGS, LIVING AND DEAD.

Fi waited. The god stayed silent. Guess that was a no, then.

YOU WILL NOT FAIL.

"Is that a prophecy?" Fi asked, hope lacing her voice. Maybe gods could see the future, like psychics.

Arawn stared unblinking at them. YOU WILL NOT FAIL BECAUSE YOU CANNOT FAIL. I CAN MAINTAIN THE BARRIER FOR NOW, BUT THE LONGER THIS CONTINUES, THE MORE POWER IT WILL TAKE AND THE WEAKER I WILL BECOME. IT HAS ALREADY BEGUN.

With a gesture, the scenery around them rippled and they were in front of a pulsing darkness. Fi took a step backwards and swore softly. It pressed on the realm, a hungry presence ready to consume. As Fi watched, it inched closer, covering the singed grass and melting it into nothingness. She retreated a few more paces.

THIS IS THE EDGE OF THE REALM OF SOULS. IF IT FAILS, THE SPIRITS WILL RETURN TO YOUR REALM.

"It will not happen," Mort said, gripping the hilt of the sword that had appeared at his waist.

Arawn inclined his head. NO, IT WILL NOT. I SHALL KEEP A CLOSE WATCH OVER YOUR PROGRESS.

With that, he vanished, leaving a portal in his wake. Mort gestured for Fi to go first, and she stumbled through, back onto the Magewell street.

"What's the big deal if souls come back to earth? They're ghosts, right? It's not like they can hurt anyone."

"Not all souls are benign, Fi. And not all spirits are human. You've got a donkey possessed by a demon living in your back garden, now imagine if that was a person he had possessed. How much harm could they do? The balance would be irrevocably broken and…I don't know what would happen or if it could ever be put right."

"But if it's so bad, why can't Arawn just come to this realm and help."

"There are rules. Gods used to roam the earth alongside mortals, many thousands of years ago, but it got…messy."

"You mean all those myths are real?"

"Part of them is."

"Huh. I always thought it was rubbish told by people who were either high or drunk."

Mort gave her a look.

"What? They didn't drink water back then so they were all half cut on beer or wine."

"Well, it's true." Mort folded his arms. "What are we going to do?"

"First thing tomorrow, we'll look into Kite's contacts. Larry's sorting out an ID for the curry house zombie and we know that it's someone who can travel between Omensford and Magewell."

"OK." He dragged his hand through his dark hair. "So, do you want to come over tonight? I can get us a takeaway."

"I don't think that's a good idea. I'd better write this up and you have work tomorrow."

His face fell. Fi's stomach clenched. She hated hurting him, but she needed space to think and she should write a report on this. She did not want the unspoken question hanging over them all night.

"You can tell me what you're thinking, you know," Mort said.

That I'm scared you're going to propose. "It's nothing."

"It's not nothing. You've got that look on your face when you're overthinking something." He gave her a lopsided smile and tucked a strand of hair behind her ear.

"It's just the case."

He sighed and removed his hand. "OK. Don't tell me. I'll give you a lift back home."

"Mort…"

He shook his head and strode to his car. Fi sighed and followed after. This was why she hated relationships. She was so bad at them, always hurting the other person with her inept social skills. In the car, she hunched against the passenger seat and kept quiet, curling her hands into fists so she didn't tap her fingers against her legs. She wished she could sink into the chair and disappear. Her magic built beneath her skin as her emotions spiralled and she gazed unseeing into the deep darkness of the countryside at night as it sped past.

They reached Omensford without saying a word.

"See you tomorrow then. Call me if you find anything." Mort stared straight ahead out of the windscreen.

Fi leaned over and pressed her lips to his cheek. "Tomorrow."

As she walked up the path to the back door, her eyes filled with tears.

Chapter 21

By the time she'd walked the length of the garden, her tears were hot, and anger bubbled in her chest. Why did Mort get to decide the pace of their relationship? What kind of person asked someone to marry them without hinting first? A selfish one, that's who. They didn't even live together. Nobody got married before living together. It was the twenty first century, for goddess' sake.

Fi slammed the door behind her. Well, she tried to slam it, but the house had an aversion to that action and refused, instead closing the door gently. Very unsatisfying. She stamped over to the kitchen and grabbed a ceramic mixing bowl from the cupboard.

What happened to you? Bad date?

"Something like that."

If you're cooking, you couldn't make me some bacon, could you?

"I'm not in the mood for your attitude."

I do not have an attitude. You're the one stress baking.

"Yeah, well. I'm stressed and I need sugar and calories." Fi popped a chocolate chip into her mouth as she spoke. Tonight, scones just weren't going to cut it. She needed chocolate. Fi chucked ingredients into the bowl and mixed them together so vigorously her arm hurt. She had long given up on electric food processors that shorted out when her magic swelled with her emotions. Besides, mixing by hand was good for working out the stress.

Wait a minute. Cressida sniffed at Fi's converse trainers. *What's that smell?*

"Have I stepped in something?"

No. It's strange…

Fi swallowed and stopped stirring. "It might be from the other realm."

What?!

"A portal just appeared. I had to go–"

You went to the other realm without me. Again.

"Sorry."

Honestly, I cannot leave you alone, can I? From now on, I go wherever you go.

"Brilliant. A wyrm babysitter."

Cressida stayed silent, regarding Fi with suspicious green eyes.

Fi dolloped blobs of the cookie mix onto a baking tray and chucked it into the oven before striding over to the chest freezer and retrieving a tub of ice cream.

She took a large spoonful, and it was halfway to her mouth before her mother walked into the kitchen, planner under one arm, cane in the other hand.

"Fiona, use a bowl, would you?"

Fi huffed out a long-suffering sigh and got a bowl from the cupboard. She scooped a generous amount of ice cream into it, covering the cat pattern etched onto the bottom and met her mother's gaze as she returned the tub to the freezer. "Happy now?"

"Thank you. Now, what is going on? I had a call from Colin about a magical disturbance tonight."

"Who's Colin?"

"The Chair of the Magewell WWWI branch." Her mother's impatience hung on every word. "So, was there a disturbance?"

"Oh. There was."

"And?"

"And the necromancer raised another zombie – identity currently unknown – and then the God of Death told me to hurry up, and I didn't even pick up my curry and now I have to go and write this up and find a lead or else I might not last the week. So, if you don't mind, I think I'll wait for the cookies to bake then head upstairs."

On cue, the oven beeped and she retrieved the cookies, piled five on top of the ice cream, took a bite out of a sixth, burning her mouth, and headed up to her room.

Behind her, her mother muttered, "I only asked." Nell raised her voice. "And I assume you're not joining us for family games in the living room?"

Fi didn't bother to reply.

Chapter 22

The first thing Fi heard the next morning was her sister's voice. Next to her bed. She rubbed the sleep out of her eyes.

"Fi…something's going on with this gnome."

Why is your sister interrupting my sleep?

Fi stroked Cressida's scaly head in sympathy – at least her familiar was talking to her again – and tried to catch up with her sister's words. "What do you mean?"

"It's moved. Again. And Bea and Neville swear they didn't do it."

"What do you want me to do, Aggy?"

"Investigate it! You're the Magical Liaison Office agent, aren't you?"

"It's a garden gnome."

Agatha twisted a gardening glove in one hand. "Please, Fi."

"Fine. If it's bothering you that much, I'll stake out the garden."

Agatha leapt at her sister and wrapped her arms around her neck. "Thank you, oh, thank you."

"But you owe me."

Her sister gave her a final hug and flounced out of the room. Fi slumped back down on the bed. Her stomach gave a warning roll. She'd eaten too much sugar and not enough proper food last night, and the energy drink hadn't helped, and then her friends hadn't even been online so she'd had to team up with some teenagers in Overwatch, never a fun experience, even with a voice modulator so they didn't know she was female.

With a groan, she heaved herself out of bed and went downstairs. Cressida followed, her nostrils quivering at the rich, salty scent of bacon wafting through the house. Her mother was up.

Fi headed straight for the pan on the stove. Her mother's walking stick thwacked her on the back of her hand.

"Ow!" She rubbed her injury and snatched her hand away.

"This is for our guest. You can make breakfast after."

"Guest? I thought they all left yesterday."

"Someone turned up last night. Aaron De'ath. I wondered if he was any relation to your doctor."

"Hmmm." A suspicion started to form in Fi's mind. "Shall I take the breakfast through?"

"That's very helpful of you…"

Fi gave her mother a beaming smile and scooped the bacon onto a plate next to a fried egg, beans and a hash brown. Her stomach growled, but she ignored it and swept across the kitchen and the hall to the B&B dining room.

A tall man sat at one of the tables, reading a paper. She plonked the plate on the table in front of him.

"Arawn?" she asked.

He put the paper down, revealing a handsome face with an angular chin and bright green eyes. In the blink of an eye, his head morphed into the creepy skull, complete with horns, then it was back to a more human form. He gave her a wink and eyed the breakfast.

WON'T YOU JOIN ME FOR BREAKFAST?

"Mort said you couldn't cross into our realm."

I CHOOSE NOT TO. THINGS WERE COMPLICATED WHEN GODS WALKED WITH MANKIND. BUT, I THINK I NEED TO PAY CLOSER ATTENTION TO YOUR INVESTIGATION, SO I WILL STAY HERE UNTIL THE NECROMANCER IS APPREHENDED.

"Great."

I WILL BE DISCREET.

"Sure. Can you sense anything now you're in our realm? Any idea where the evil magic user is?"

IT DOESN'T WORK LIKE THAT. YOU WILL REPORT BACK TO ME EVERY EVENING AND I WILL SHARE ANY INFORMATION I FIND.

"You're not shadowing me?"

I HAVE MY OWN AVENUES OF INVESTIGATION.

"And they are?"

I WILL INFORM YOU IF I FIND ANYTHING.

"Super. Anything else?"

DO YOU HAVE ANY HP SAUCE?

Fi got him his sauce and sat down in the kitchen with a bacon sandwich. Now she had a god staying in her mother's B&B and a necromancer on the loose. How could things get worse? Cressida sat next to her, eating charred bacon from a plain plate.

You're annoyed.

"No, I'm not."

I can feel it. It's...

"Annoying?"

Yes. You need to let off some steam.

Maybe her familiar was right. She finished her sandwich, licked the remnants of the glorious bacon grease from her fingers and headed outside.

Chapter 23

Fi's brow beaded with sweat as she stared at the ball of electricity in her hand. With an effort of will, she shaped the blue-white sphere it into a cube and flattened it, before adding details. She held it out in front of her, unable to keep the smile from her face.

"What do you think?"

If you were aiming for a box, you succeeded.

"A box? This is a Nintendo sixty-four – my first gaming console. See, there's the logo."

Very nice.

"There's no need for sarcasm." With a sigh, Fi hefted the electrical console at the singed log that took the brunt of her practice sessions.

No, I can see how, if you need to attack something, then taking the time to fashion a computer before lobbing it at something will be very useful.

"First, it's not a computer; it's a games console. What would you prefer? A dagger made of electricity?" Fi shaped a dagger from her magic and hurled it at the log. It fizzled out on contact with the blackened wood. "Second, I want to get more control of my magic, so I don't have to lob it at people."

Well done.

Fi nodded to her familiar, that almost sounded genuine. She concentrated on shaping a PlayStation next, but it fizzled out as her phone rang, distracting her.

"Hello?"

"Ledd here. I've got something on Kite. Want to join me?"

"Sure."

She noted down the address; not too far from her home.

"See you in fifteen." He hung up.

"Come on, Cressida, we've got some detecting to do."

Seventeen minutes later, Fi saw Detective Ledd's Fiat parked up outside a non-descript semi-detached house. It was the usual buttery yellow of Cotswolds stone and the garden was colourful but overgrown. The detective stood outside the wooden door waving a key. Fi hurried up the path of round stones, laid in a curving route through the front lawn and joined him.

"About time."

"I had to walk across the village."

"I thought you passed your test."

"I don't have a car."

The detective snorted and unlocked the door with a flourish. "Mr Kite's home. Let's take a look around."

He led the way inside and Fi followed, her feet springing on the spongy carpet. "You take the upstairs, I'll take the downstairs?" she said.

"And I'll be in Scotland afore ye."

"What?"

"The song. Loch Lomond? Peter Hollins? I thought you were…never mind." He disappeared upstairs muttering about young people and their lack of musical taste between panting breaths.

Fi thought it was a compliment to be considered young when she was over thirty. She started with the kitchen. It was sparse; cooker, microwave, small table. Patterned linoleum covered the floor, practical but it made Fi's eyes hurt to look at it for too long. She opened a couple of cupboards and found row after row of tins and a stack of plates. Nothing personal. She looked in the fridge out of curiosity and took in the neatly stacked ready meals. He wasn't expecting to die, but then, no one did.

Cressida sniffed around the room. *It's clean, at least.*

Fi inhaled the fresh scent of lemons with an undertone of bleach. Clean alright. Did he always live like this, or did someone clean up after they killed him? She shut the fridge and headed for the room next to it; a dining room with a formal dark-wood table and six matching chairs. Framed prints of famous pictures of fruit hung on the walls. It had the musty smell of a room seldom used.

Her familiar flicked her tongue, scenting the air, and shook her head. Fi closed the door. Nothing to see in there.

The final room downstairs was a lounge. This had more personality. A pile of motor magazines lay on a small side table next to a large, special support chair that allowed the sitter to get up with the press of a button. It looked comfy, maybe her mum would like a mobility chair. She voiced the thought aloud and Cressida barked out a laugh.

I want to be there when you suggest that.

"What? She's got that cane now, she's getting on a bit."

Please let me be there. You'll want someone to witness your murder.

The scrape of a key in the front door stopped Fi's reply. She popped her head out of the lounge door and caught Larry's eye as he peered down the stairs. The detective motioned to Fi to hide and she crouched by the sofa while he took up a position in the kitchen.

Fi's heart raced as the intruder entered with soft footsteps, barely audible on the carpeted entranceway. Fi gripped the arm of the sofa. The steps came closer. Fi closed her eyes and reached out with her magic, sensing the electricity that pulsed through any living being.

Only one person, but why were they moving like that? To her heightened senses, the figure swayed and spun in a electrical light show of nerve endings. She made herself smaller as the person sashayed towards the lounge.

Chapter 24

"Halt," Detective Ledd's voice came down the hall. The figure ignored him and twirled into the lounge.

Fi opened her eyes. A curvy lady swayed her bottom and called out. "Kenneth, it's Janine, let me know if you need any assistance."

The woman turned, saw Fi crouching like some sort of crazy goblin by the sofa and screamed. Fi shrieked in response and stood, her bottom knocking a table and sending a photo frame crashing to the ground.

The woman took out her headphones and held out a bottle of cleaning fluid like a weapon. "Who are you and where's Kenneth?"

The detective appeared behind her. "Put down the spray."

She screamed again and whirled, spraying antibacterial liquid into the detective's face. He cursed and pressed his fingers to his eyes.

Fi took a step forward. "It's OK, he's a detective, with the police, and I'm part of the Magical Liaison Office." She held up her ID and the woman peered at it.

"The police?"

"I'm guessing no one told you about Mr Kite?"

"No, why? Is he in trouble?"

"Er, yes…no…he's dead."

"Dead?" Janine echoed Fi's word back to her and collapsed into the nearest seat, the bottle fell to the floor, forgotten.

Fi nodded. The detective might have words with her later about her lack of tact, but, given he was blustering around, screeching about his eyes, he didn't have much say in the matter.

"Stay there for a minute." Fi left the cleaner in the chair and led the detective to the kitchen where she soaked a tea towel in cold water for him. She made a cup of tea using the bags in the cupboard and checked the milk. That was what you did when people were in shock, right? Make tea.

"Hope you like it black," she said as she brought in a steaming mug from the kitchen.

Janine took it and nodded, staring unseeing at the net curtains. Fi left her be and picked up pieces of shattered glass from the picture frame. A frown creased her forehead. The man in the picture with the deceased was familiar…Fi snapped a photo while the woman was distracted and put the rest of the broken frame into the bin.

As she sipped, the woman's pallor returned, and her eyes brightened. Maybe there was something in the old adage about tea in times of crisis.

"What was that stuff?" The detective entered the room, blinking as tears streamed down his face.

"Oh, that's my homemade cleaner. All natural ingredients. It's better than the weak stuff you get in the shops."

"Stronger, certainly. Do I need to go to hospital?"

"Oh, no, child, you just rinse it out. But stay away from any naked flames, you hear me?"

Still winking one eye, the detective asked, "Who are you and what are you doing here?"

"I'm Janine Johnson, certified carer for Cotswolds Help and Care. We provide care and help to those who need it in the community. Mr Kite is one of my clients." She dug in her large carpet bag and pulled out a card.

The detective took it, squinted and handed it to Fi. The neat, printed card had a large sunflower on one side and Janine's name on the other.

"No one told me he'd gone, poor dear. When did he pass?"

"About four days ago."

She sucked in her cheeks and made a kissing sound. "Was it quick?"

"Er, it was a heart attack," Fi said.

"Poor man. What a thing to come back to after my holiday."

"Where did you go?" Fi asked.

The detective cut across her. "How long did you care for him?"

"Two years. He was a nice man, always cheerful, never a bother."

"And what did you do for him?"

"Oh, I helped him out, cleaned the place up, took care of the laundry, cooked – he loved my chicken and rice – and helped with his, er, cleanliness, toiletries, that sort of thing. I will miss him."

"Were any other carers assigned to him?"

"No, we have our own individuals, it helps with the personal touch. I came here five days every week for two years." That far off look came into her eyes again. "Was he at home, when it happened?"

"Er, not sure."

I can't smell anything apart from bleach. And the detective's cologne.

Fi sniffed. He was a bit pungent, and it didn't mix well with whatever was in the homemade cleaning spray. The detective swayed on his feet.

"Well, I'd better get him somewhere with better ventilation. Do you need more time?"

The lady shook her head and gulped down the remains of her tea before collecting her bag and the discarded bottle. "No, I'd better call head office and see where they want me now."

That seemed heartless, even to Fi. Janine must have seen the look on the witch's face, because she patted her arm and said,

"Child, when you're in my line of work, you deal with death or illness every day. It's always sad, but sometimes it's a blessing. Mr Kite – Kenneth – wasn't happy. He was a race car driver when he was younger, and a successful one too, he didn't like being old. He was kind enough, but you could tell, and I always counted his tablets when I was here, just in case. I don't wish death on anyone but it's not always an easy road into old age. Not everyone is surrounded by loving families at the end. Some people are alone and in pain and wish for it all to stop on their terms. He lived well, that's all any of us can ask for. Now, I'd better get on. Come on, I'll lock up."

"I will lock up," the detective said, fumbling in his pocket for the key. He led the way out. He would have seemed more in charge, had he not walked straight into the doorframe. Fi bit her lip to stop the guffaw of laughter that threatened to escape and helped him outside.

They waited for Janine to climb into her sunshine yellow VW beetle and drive off before they spoke. Detective Ledd slumped against the wall, blinking in the daylight, his eyes so red he could have stood in for a stop sign.

"I think you need to go to a hospital."

"She said it was all natural ingredients."

"Cyanide's a natural ingredient, but you'd still go to hospital if you had some sprayed in your face." Fi paused and frowned. "Well, maybe you wouldn't, maybe you'd be dead."

"Has anyone ever told you that your bedside manner leaves a lot to be desired?"

He's right.

Fi shot her familiar a look. "You don't work with me for the sympathy."

"You're right. I work with you for your expertise on magic. Any leads on the necromancer?"

"Let's get you to hospital." Fi led him to his car and waited. When he made a move to get into the driver's seat, she placed a hand on his shoulder. "I can't let you drive."

"I don't know…"

"Come on, I've passed my test. What's the worst that could happen?"

He gave her a long look before clutching his face and screwing his eyes shut.

"OK, you're right. I'll call an ambulance and we'll hope that they get here before you lose your eyesight."

"Fine," he shoved the keys into her palm and she helped him into the passenger seat before letting Cressida in the back, taking her place at the steering wheel and pulling out. "This could not have come at a worse time, I'm seeing Miranda tomorrow."

Who's Miranda? Wait. I don't care.

"The warlock?"

"She's coming to Omensford for a couple of days. I booked her a chauffeured car."

"She can't take the bus?"

"From London? I don't want her on a coach with the dregs of society."

"Hey! I take the bus."

The detective stayed silent.

"I can go off people, you know."

"Just get me to the hospital. It feels like my retinas are trying to escape through my forehead."

Fi pulled a face in sympathy and put her foot down on the accelerator.

Chapter 25

Fi sat in the waiting room, flipping through a magazine that promised to answer all her questions about PMS and show her ten different ways to use silver eyeshadow. Cressida curled around her neck, snoring softly. The receptionist had decided not to quibble about whether the wyrm fell under the remit of the 'no dogs' sign posted next to the entrance.

She gave up on the magazine – why was it always gossip magazines and never an issue of Computer Weekly? – and stared round the waiting room instead, shifting on the uncomfortable plastic chair. Tired looking people sat on carbon copies of her chair in a shade of beige that could have been called 'tea stains on a shirt'.

She tried to guess why people were here. The man with the bloodied bandage around his hand was obvious, but there was a woman in the corner who winced every time she moved. Stomach trouble, maybe?

At least the detective was already with a doctor. Larry had moaned constantly while he sat next to her, alternating whinges about the pain with heartfelt sighs followed by comments like 'I remember what it was like to see colour'.

He hadn't taken it well when she'd replied that it was just the washed-out waiting room paint that made him worry about his sight. Now he was off having an eye bath somewhere and she was stuck with out-of-date magazines.

"Here you are, sir."

Fi looked up. Larry stood in front of her, a nurse grasping his elbow and beaming.

I didn't know they were casting for The Mummy.

Fi swallowed her laugh at Cressida's catty comment.

"Your dad's all ready to go home now."

"Not my dad."

The nurse's face screwed up for a microsecond before she regained her composure.

"Not that, either. We're colleagues."

"Oh, right. Well, he's all done. No lasting damage, but keep the bandages on for twenty four hours."

"Come on then, Larry."

"It's awful, isn't it?" The detective sighed.

"No…it's fine…" She took his arm and led him out of the door into the breezy open plan carpark.

"I look like a fool. What'll I tell Miranda?"

"The bandages will be off by then."

Fi took his arm and led the detective back to his car. He gave her his address and she turned out into the traffic. The detective's hand plucked at the padding over his eyes.

"Leave it alone, you heard the nurse."

"It's torture, not being able to see."

"It'll be worse if you do yourself damage because you can't be patient. You don't want Miranda to see you like this, do you?"

He placed his hand back on his lap with a sulky "No."

Fi shook her head and turned on the radio. He swatted at her hand, missed and hit the gear stick. "Don't touch the stations."

"I'm driving, my choice of music. Get ready for best of the nineties."

"It's my car."

"Then be grateful I haven't changed your other programmes. Come on, mmm bop…"

Larry groaned and covered his ears. "Blind people have sensitive hearing, you know."

"You've developed sensitive hearing in the two hours since she sprayed you?"

"You lose one sense, the others develop. What's that smell?"

"What smell?"

He tried to tap his nose and missed. "I've got heightened senses now I've lost my sight. Something smells odd."

"It's your car."

"No, it's like bad eggs."

Cressida made a coughing sound.

"Oh, Cress, you didn't?"

It's perfectly natural.

"Right by my face? Seriously? Get in the back."

Fi gagged on the now potent aroma of sulphur and wafted one hand to clear the air before cracking the window.

Larry looked at her, two huge, white cotton pads staring from the passenger seat. "Told you. Heightened senses."

Fi drove Larry back to his house – a brick semi-detached property on the edge of Magewell, with a lawn made of bright green artificial turf – and helped him in. She walked him to the sitting room and helped him onto the leather sofa.

"OK, I'll get you some food and drink. Do you need anything else?"

"No, thanks." He squirmed on the sofa.

He needs the bathroom.

"No. Oh, no." She sent a silent prayer up to whatever gods saved people from embarrassing situations and coughed. "Do you need to…go?"

"What?"

"You know…go? To the toilet?"

He blustered something out.

"Come on then." Fi helped him up and led him to the bathroom. "But I'm not going in with you."

"I should think not."

Fi hurried back to the kitchen and made him a sandwich and a cold drink. The bathroom door banged open.

"Do you need some help?" Fi scurried back to his side.

"Of course not!" He edged down the hall and back into the lounge. Fi's head turned, drawn to the toilet like it was a car accident. Drips spackled the tiled floor. She debated cleaning up, then decided it was too disgusting and she had her own mess to tidy up at home. He could clean that up in the morning. She looked away and followed the detective into the lounge just in time to see him knock into the coffee table. He swore. She was impressed at the variety of curses he let out.

"Let me help you." She got him into the chair and set him up with the sandwich and the remote.

"What am I meant to do with this?"

Fi pulled a face. Right. He couldn't see. "Er, listen to the TV?"

"Brilliant. You could be a comedian."

"Do you need anything else?"

"I need my bloody eyesight back."

"OK, do you need anything else from me?"

"No."

"Do you want me to stay?"

"No."

"Are you sure?"

"Yes."

"OK, I'm going then."

"Good. Call me when you've got something on the case."

Fi's shoulders sagged with relief as soon as she was the other side of the neat, UPVC front door. "That was close."

You almost had to take care of someone. Oh no.

"I've already got one grump to take care of."

Are you referring to me?

Her phone blared out the Gardener's World theme tune, saving her from answering her familiar.

"Are you coming over?" Agatha sounded excited.

"Huh?"

"To stake out the gnome mover."

"Oh…right…I'm sort of in the middle of a case."

"Now?"

"I suppose not right now."

"Great, then you can come over. See you soon." Her sister hung up.

Fi let out a sigh. "Fancy gnome watching with me, Cress?"

Cressida. And someone had better come with you, or who knows what trouble you'll get into.

"That's not fair. It's not like I go out looking for trouble."

And yet, it finds you.

Fi couldn't argue with that. She bent for her familiar to climb up on her shoulders before heading to the bus stop. Somehow, she didn't think that the detective would be happy lending her his car.

Chapter 26

"Cake?" Agatha asked.

"Go on then." Fi accepted the proffered slice, served on a chipped plate.

If you keep eating like that, you won't be able to fit into your trousers.

"That's what leggings are for."

"Hmm?" Agatha asked, unable to hear Cressida's psychic snark.

"Oh, Cressida's just telling me to stop eating cake."

"I wish I had a voice in my head that told me to stop eating cake."

"Believe me, you don't. Ouch!"

Oops.

Fi rubbed her leg where the wyrm's claws had dug in.

"I'm thinking of joining one of those slimming clubs."

"Aggy, you do not need to join a fat club."

"What do you know? You're all skin and bones. It'll catch up with you, though. As soon as you get over thirty-five, your metabolism slows down and the calories sneak on your thighs. Either that or someone's made my clothes shrink."

Fi rolled her eyes at her sister.

If she wants to lose weight, why doesn't she just exercise?

"Cressida asks why you can't exercise."

"Well that's part of the problem, isn't it? Where am I meant to find the time between working and looking after Bea and running this house and the garden? If I don't keep on top of it, the dandelions and snapdragons will take over the place. And, besides, what can I do? There's nothing for women of a certain age."

"Aggy, you are not of a certain age."

"I am. And I don't want to wear Lycra, so yoga's out, what else is there?"

Tennis? Football?

"Stop listing sports you watch on TV," Fi snapped at her familiar.

"See, it's hopeless. I was thinking about running, but I don't want to go on my own…"

Offer to go with her, you could use the exercise.

"Cheeky." Fi drummed her fingers on the windowsill. It couldn't hurt to get into shape. Who knew when she might next be sucked through a portal to a death maze. "Fine. Agatha, would you like me to go jogging with you?"

"Oh, Fi. Would you? Really?"

"Yes," Fi said through gritted teeth. "But I don't do mornings. Now, didn't you say something about pizza?"

"Pizza?"

"It's not a proper stakeout without pizza. That's like police rules." Fi's phone rang and she grabbed for it in her pocket. "I'll have pepperoni. Hello?"

"Fi? How are you?" Mort's voice sent a warm shiver down her spine.

"Good, good. You?" She pushed the net curtains to one side for a better view of the garden. Her sister bustled out of the room to give her some privacy.

"I'm fine. Do you fancy coming over tonight? We could have some dinner, watch some TV…"

"That sounds perfect, but I can't. I'm gnome watching with Agatha."

"Gnome watching?"

"Don't ask."

"I thought we could work on the case together. And maybe…talk."

"About that…Arawn's at Mum's."

There was a long silence.

"Hello? Are you still there?" Fi asked.

"Yes. I thought you said that the God of Death was with your mum."

"He is. He said he'd stay while the necromancer was still at large."

"But he never comes into the mortal realm."

"Well, he has."

Mort swore. "Dad'll have a field day with this. First time in family history that he's crossed over and it's on my watch. Sometimes I wish I had a different vocation."

"Maybe you could talk to him, tell him how you feel."

"Tell the God of Death I want to leave his service, you mean?"

"When you put it like that…"

The irony of you talking about feelings is delicious. Cressida stretched.

"Give me a minute." She put the phone against her chest. "What's that supposed to mean?"

You never talk about your feelings, you bottle them up until you explode something.

"I…" Fi trailed off.

Exactly.

"So, you think I should marry him."

Cressida scoffed. *No. You're nowhere near the level of maturity it requires for that level of commitment.*

"What then?"

Just tell Mort that you're not ready for marriage. He'll understand.

"Since when are you an expert on relationships?"

Cressida flicked her tail and gave Fi a look.

"Sorry about that, Mort, I'm back. So, it's a no go on speaking to Arawn?"

"I don't think so." He sighed and Fi's stomach plunged. She hadn't realised he felt so badly about working for the god. "Any news on the case?"

"I went to Kite's place today. But there was nothing there. It was clean. No break in. No evidence of a murder."

"So it was natural causes?"

"Looks that way, but no idea how they got his body out of the house…"

"Maybe he went for a walk?"

"His carer didn't seem to think he was that mobile…"

"What about the other guy?"

"Nothing yet…sorry, Mort, got to go. I'll call you tomorrow." Fi hung up and stared out of the window at the small shape making its way across the lawn.

Chapter 27

Fi pulled back the curtain further and filmed the small figure. It was dark, but it looked like a sizeable garden gnome waddling across the lawn to the flowerbed.

"Aggy?" Fi said. When there was no reply, she shouted, "Aggy?"

"Keep it down, Fi. Bea's sleeping. Or at least, she was."

Fi pointed out of the window and Agatha sidled up beside her. Agatha's jaw dropped. "Is that…?"

"Have you got any outside lights?"

Her sister nodded and led the way downstairs.

"Evening ladies," Neville said from the table as they passed him.

"Nice army, Nev."

"Thanks, Fi, I call them the–"

"No time, we're gnome hunting."

Still filming, Fi angled her phone camera through the patio door glass. "Cut the inside lights."

Agatha turned them off, then hurried over to the switch for the outdoor lights.

"Ready?" Fi asked.

Agatha nodded.

"Now."

Agatha pressed the switch and the outside lights blared on, flooding the lawn in garish white.

Both sisters pressed their noses against the window. There, on the lawn, was a garden gnome, frozen in mid-step.

Agatha elbowed Fi in the ribs. "Told you there was something going on with my gnome."

Fi closed her mouth, still filming.

"What's the plan?"

"Er, the plan." That's right, she was the Magical Liaison Office Community Agent. She ought to know what to do in these situations, even if there was nothing in the handbook for dealing with the night of the living gnomes. "Let's go and talk to it. Make contact." That sounded official.

"Right." Agatha grabbed her gardening gloves and hat.

"What's that for?"

"In case he bites."

"And the hat?"

"Oh, habit." Agatha removed the flowery sun hat from her head and placed her hand on the key in the lock. At a nod from Fi, she unlocked the door and the sisters charged screaming into the back garden.

They stopped two feet from the unmoving gnome.

Very impressive.

"Shut up, Cressida."

No, very good. You scared him to stone.

Fi rubbed the back of her neck and crouched down. At eye level, the gnome had an expression between fear and determination that she was sure hadn't been on his face when she'd picked him. His clothes were less bright too, as if someone had scrubbed at the luminous paintjob.

"OK, Gnomeo. The jig's up. We know you're alive."

The gnome stayed still.

"How do we get him to move?" Agatha asked.

Fi poked him with her toe. The gnome clutched her foot and heaved, pushing her off balance. She tumbled onto the soft lawn and the gnome legged it towards the flower beds. Fi scrambled upright and sprinted after him, diving on top of the hard creature. He kicked and punched in her grip, knocking her jaw with a fist that felt like stone. Her teeth clacked together, and, with a cry, she dropped him.

On instinct, she aimed a small ball of electricity at the gnome, but it crackled over him without slowing him down.

Cressida weaved her way across the grass and breathed a ball of fire at the small gnome. He rolled and ducked into a bushy plant with broad leaves.

"Grab him!" Fi shouted.

Agatha shoved her gloved hands under the bush and brought out the gnome, dangling by one leg. He twisted in her grip, but this was a woman who could snap through inch thick rose stems with secateurs, and she held on.

Fi rubbed her jaw and planted herself opposite him. "Who are you?"

"Let me go!"

"What are you?"

"Put me down!"

She grabbed his pointed hat to stop him squirming in Agatha's grasp and looked him straight in his beady eyes. "Tell us everything or Agatha here will let her daughter give you a new paint job."

"You wouldn't!" The gnome twitched.

"I got her glow in the dark paint for Christmas," Fi said with a glint in her eye.

He sagged. "Alright, but put me down and I'll tell you."

Fi nodded to her sister and Agatha placed him on the damp grass. A cage of thick stems grew around him, trapping him in one spot. When they started to bloom, Fi put a hand on Agatha's arm. "That's enough, Aggy. He's not going anywhere."

"Right," she said, shaking her hand. "Got a bit carried away."

Fi took a knee in front of the organic jail cell. "So, who are you?"

Chapter 28

The small gnome inhaled deeply. "My name is Priapus, and I am king of the rock gnomes."

"Rock gnomes?"

His eyes thundered for a split second before he leaned on the rosewood bars and folded his arms. "I wouldn't expect you to know about us. We keep ourselves secret, ever since the thirties."

"What happened in the thirties?"

He met her gaze. "Snow White and the Seven Dwarves."

"The film?"

He shuddered. "It was bad enough when the warlocks Grimm wrote it, but this was a new level. Ever since then, my people have been in hiding."

"But I found you in a garden centre."

"Yes. Centuries of evolution have given us the ability to transform into stone when confronted with a threat. Throughout history, it's worked and we've been nothing more than statues passing through a garden. But since that film…gnomes are popular. It's sickening. Unscrupulous humans find us sometimes and put us in their gardens." He paused to glare at the sisters from between the winding bars of his prison. "Normally, we can escape, but this time…they took everyone. All my people stuck in that jail. They painted us." He banged on the bars. "I had a plan to break us out, and find a new home, then some idiot bought me."

"That would be you." Agatha beamed at her sister.

"Thanks, Aggy."

"I have to get back to my people."

"Where will you go?"

He shrugged and picked a piece of paint. "We have no home. But we'll find somewhere."

Agatha and Fi shared a look.

"There's no place like gnome."

"They want to get a gnome in the country."

"Show me the way to go gnome."

"They're gnome-ads."

Both sisters burst into giggles.

"I'm glad you find this funny. My people are stuck in a glass jail and you're laughing."

Fi wiped a tear from her eye. "Sorry, you're right. It's serious. But it's not a jail, it's a garden centre. We can get them for you."

"Really?"

"Of course. It's the least I can do, seeing as I, you know, bought you."

"And until you find somewhere new, you can stay in my garden," Agatha said. "I'll put some extra protection spells around it."

"Thank you."

Agatha waved her hand in a graceful arc and the branches that held the gnome captive sank back into the soil.

Fi held out her hand for the gnome to shake. He looked at it, then up at her then shook it, squeezing hard. "Swear it."

Fi held up her free hand. "I swear we will get your people from the garden centre."

He released her and nodded. "Now, can I get a wire brush? This paint is murder to get off."

Agatha bustled away to find him something to scrub with, and they left the gnome in the dark with a basin of soapy water.

"Well, that was weird."

"Trust you to pick an endangered species for my birthday present. Can I see the video?"

Fi handed over her phone.

Agatha swiped through the pictures. "Hang on. Why have you got a picture of Quentin on your phone?"

"Who?"

Agatha turned the phone and pointed to the image of the man dressed in black next to Mr Kite. "Quentin. He's one of our tutors – one of the best, actually – he's training Diane right now. He was at my party."

"So that's where I recognised him from." Mr Creepy looked different when he wasn't all in black. "I need to speak to him about necromancy."

Chapter 29

Fi strode into the school with Agatha at her side the following morning.

"I still don't understand why you think Quentin knows anything about necromancy."

Fi raised an eyebrow at her sister. Had Agatha not seen the guy? He dressed in black. With a cloak. Prime necromancer material. But she said, "It's important I talk to anyone who might have known Kite, and they're in a picture together."

"I suppose, but I've known him for years and I trust him."

"Like Sam Hackett?"

Agatha's face paled at the mention of the deceased PE teacher. "That was different."

Fi supposed it was different. After all, Sam had been murdered, but after his death, she'd found out he was a member of the Anti-Magic League, an organisation that did not think mundanes and magical beings should live in harmony together. If the press was to be believed, they were behind the bigger and more violent protests against magical beings that had ramped up since the dragons had been revived.

Her magic itched under her skin just thinking about some of the hatred she'd read in the online chatrooms. "Just let me do my job."

"Fine, but don't bully him."

"Bully?" Fi said, but Agatha was gone.

Fi fumed in the corridor. It was rich of Agatha to speak of bullying. Her sister had fitted in at school, had plenty of friends, been invited to parties. Fi was the one who stood alone at the edge of the playground, until a teacher had let her use the computer lab during breaks.

Calm down. Cressida shifted on her shoulders. *You're making me anxious.*

With some effort, Fi pushed aside the childhood memories and marched to the office.

The hall was painted the same shade of murky green she remembered. If the decorator had been aiming for uplifting, they'd missed the mark by several shades. Even the smell was the same; bleach with an undertone of pencils and, for some reason, urine.

Fi forced herself to take even breaths. She wasn't a teenager anymore. This place didn't have power over her as an adult.

"Could I speak to Quentin Lenoir, please?" Her voice came out an octave higher than usual and she coughed before repeating her request.

The chirpy lady behind the desk smiled. "Fi, isn't it? Agatha's sister? We met at her party."

"Oh, yes." Fi gave a weak smile in return. "Nice to see you again." What was her name? Fi's gaze raked the desk taking in a photo of the woman beaming next to a younger man – her son? Or husband? – the neat stacks of paperwork, the business card from some Sunflower Agency, and came to rest on the name badge: Harriet Still.

Harriet – Hetty, that was it – followed her gaze. "My son, Liam. Gorgeous, isn't he? He goes everywhere with me, bless his soul." Her lips tilted upwards in a wistful smile. "So, is he in trouble?"

"Who?" How would Fi know if this lady's son was in trouble?

"Quentin Lenoir."

"Oh, no, I just need to speak with him for my enquiries on a case."

"A case." She clapped her hands. "How exciting. What's it about?"

"I can't say."

"I see. Let me check the timetable…here we are, he's teaching the year twelves at the moment. I'll take you there, it's almost break time." She pressed some buttons on a keypad to release the office door, and joined Fi in the hall.

"More security than when I went here," Fi said, gesturing to the keypad.

"Oh yes, it's all changed since then. Every time the agency sends me here, something's new."

"Agency?"

"I temp for a few places, don't like to be tied down. I'm sorry, but we don't allow animals in school."

Cressida hissed.

"She's my familiar, Cressida."

Introduce me with my full name.

Fi sighed. "Lady Cressida Charmington."

"No familiars either. Sorry. The school's quite strict, otherwise pupils bring in all sorts of animals claiming they're familiars. You can chain her up outside."

Excuse me.

"Maybe you can just wait by the doors, Cressida."

I don't want to leave you alone. What if you disappear to another realm again? Cressida shifted on Fi's shoulders.

"I'll be fine. And if a portal opens, I'll come back for you. Happy?"

No. But Cressida stalked outside and sat on her haunches by the door.

Great. Fi was going to have to deal with one grumpy wyrm later. Maybe steak would help.

"Follow me." The woman led the way back along the corridor to the older part of the building. "Of course, it doesn't surprise me that you're talking to him, he's always had an interest in the darker side of magic. I don't know why he's still allowed to teach after the incident."

"Incident?"

"Don't you know? The board hushed it up at the private school but one of the pupils started animating dead frogs in the science class and then someone ended up dead."

"And he did that?"

"How do you think the child learned about it?" She gave Fi a meaningful look. "Well, here you are." She knocked on the door and opened it. "Fiona Blair to see you. From the Magical Liaison Office." With that, Hetty walked back down the corridor, hips swinging in time with her steps.

Quentin Lenoir gave Fi a long appraising stare. "I will speak with you at break time. You may take a seat until then." He motioned to the back of the class and Fi slunk past the rows of watching teenagers to the free desk. She sat down and shrank as much as she could, avoiding the curious eyes that stared at her.

Fi tried to look like a grown up in control as her heart rate rocketed and she fought the urge to revert to her shy, awkward teenage self.

"Now, class, after that interruption, we shall get back to our Advanced Magic Theory lesson. Who can tell me about the classes of magic users?"

Fi scanned the classroom as the children parroted answers to the teacher. "Witches, warlocks, wizards."

"And which of these is the most powerful?"

"Witches?" a child said, raising their hand.

The ghost of a smile tugged at the corner of Quentin's mouth. "Are you asking or telling me?"

"Telling?"

"And why witches?"

"Witches are able to channel magical energy and bend it to their will."

"But only according to their natural leanings. Nature witches, for example, can manipulate plants and the earth, with some specialisms into, say, weather. But a nature witch can never use a different type of magic, only learn to channel their own power."

"Warlocks then."

"Raise your hand, Gibson. Warlocks are more versatile because their magic is learned and created through experimentation. They are less bound than other magic users, but in their own way, they are limited by their experimentation. They draw magic from their internal well and shape it in any way they choose, but, they take longer to replenish their internal magic stores than witches."

"Then it must be wizards, sir."

"Wizards learn from scrolls and books. Their control of magic is dependent on their minds, and in that way, their power is only limited by the mind. So, yes, I would say that of the three base classes of human magic users, they are the most powerful." To illustrate his point, he created a shower of sparks from his fingers with a word.

"But, of course, any of these can have exceptional power. And what are these exceptional men and women known as?"

"Sorcerers and mages."

"Good."

"What about dark magic, sir? You know, blood magic."

Fi sat straighter at her desk and kept her eyes on the teacher. His face flushed and his eyes gleamed. "Blood magic is a dangerous thing, very difficult to control and addictive. Many a magic user has fallen prey to its seduction. But it has no place in my classroom…until next term."

Nervous laughter trickled around the room. The bell sounded and the pupils shut their textbooks with claps of paper thudding together and scraped their chairs back.

Quentin raised his voice to be heard over the din of children packing up. "Your homework is to write an essay on the different ways magic can crossover and at what point an ordinary magic user can be classed as a sorcerer or mage."

He cleaned the board as the class emptied before turning to Fi. "I believe you wanted to speak with me?"

Chapter 30

Fi got to her feet. She aimed for cool MLO agent, but the effect was somewhat ruined when she banged her elbow on the hard wooden table. Rubbing her numb arm, she faced down the teacher.

"You know about blood magic?"

"Of course. As a teacher, I have to be aware of all types of magic. It's my duty to mould young minds into strong magic users so they can fulfil their potential."

"And dark magic makes you strong?"

He regarded her for several long moments before he replied. "Dark magic is a seductress that promises much and offers very little. One might think they have great powers, but soon the magic demands more and more for lower and lower returns. Take compulsion as an example. Something very few magic users are able to do successfully, but with blood magic, it becomes much easier, for a time. Before too long, the magic user is unable to tell what is right and wrong, and instead

164

focuses on getting the same or bigger results, but the price is always higher."

"You sound like you're talking from experience," Fi said, angling for some sort of confession that he used that type of magic.

"There are very few of us who have not experienced the evils of dark magic. If you are one such person, then consider yourself lucky."

Fi didn't want to dwell on her experiences of dark magic. Since starting as a Community Agent, she'd seen more murders than she'd like and a demon almost enter the world, although technically the demon now possessed a donkey in her mother's garden, so maybe he was in the world. She shook her head. That line of thinking could drive a person mad. "Where were you on Saturday?"

"Saturday…I was at your sister's party."

"Before the party."

"I was at home, getting ready."

"And home is?"

"Do you know Hallow's Boarding School?"

Fi nodded. Everyone knew the prestigious boarding school that taught the progenies of elite magical families from across Britain.

"Teachers board there as well. It helps us keep an eye on the pupils and allows for extra tuition, if needed."

"Why teach here then?" Omensford secondary school was decent enough for magical beings, but it wasn't in the same league as the boarding school just outside the town.

He gave her a thin-lipped smile that didn't expose any teeth. "I want to give back to the community."

Fi couldn't keep the look of disbelief off her face.

"This may surprise you, Ms Blair, but I am not part of the magical elite. I grew up in a council estate outside Liverpool where I saw people with talent descend into crime, and too often they took the easy way out, accepting darker magic into their lives for the promise of quick results. But, it's like a drug, and, as with any substance abuse, it left them unable to function without it.

"I saw too many friends head down that path, and, I confess, I became obsessed with learning everything I could about blood magic. So, when I passed my exams and got into university, I vowed that I would help as many young people as possible avoid that fate. It is my calling to teach magic, the proper way. To help young minds fulfil their potential, and warn them of the dangers of the easy way."

"But there was dark magic at the boarding school, wasn't there?"

A shadow passed over his face. He turned back to the clean whiteboard. "That was a long time ago. It remains one of the biggest regrets of my life."

"So, you were involved?"

"I found them. They were covered in blood. They'd sacrificed one of their friends for the power, and then added their own blood. It was my fault."

"You taught them how to use blood magic."

"No!" He whirled round, full of righteous anger before his shoulders slumped and he sank into his chair. "I should have spotted the signs. The sudden increase in magical ability, the hunger for more power, the anger when they didn't get it. And the withdrawal from others. By the time I formed my suspicions, it was already too late. The school didn't want to know – afraid it would ruin their special reputation – but I couldn't let it go.

"I followed them one Friday night, found their secret lair – an abandoned folly on school grounds. Little Yusef bleeding out in the centre of a circle and the rest of them writhing as the power consumed them. I got him to hospital…but I had to look the family in the eye and tell them I was too late." He trailed off and stared out of the window.

"Why did you keep teaching?"

He watched the children playing outside, and Fi was about to repeat her question when he spoke. "I made a promise that I would never let that happen again. That's why I tutor and teach at the state school. I have to see as many children as possible and make sure none of them are turning to the darker side of magic."

"I want the names of anyone who saw you in the couple of days before Agatha's party."

He rubbed his forehead. "You want me to give you an alibi. What is this about?"

"Quentin, does this man look familiar to you?" Fi held up her phone and showed him the picture of him and Mr Kite.

"Kenneth? Yes, of course."

"Aha."

"He's my uncle – technically my step uncle from my mother's second marriage. Why?"

"Oh." Fi made a note of the connection on her phone. It seemed odd that he wouldn't show up in the police file, but then maybe they didn't go as far as step nephews from previous marriages. She met his gaze and watched him closely. "He's dead."

Quentin sank back against the chalkboard, his face pale and slack. Fi bit her lip. People could lie, but this seemed like genuine shock, and she regretted her bluntness.

"Can I get you anything?" she asked.

"No…just give me a minute. This is…"

"Sit."

He sank into the chair with a sigh and gripped the arms until his knuckles stood out. His head whipped up. "You think I have something to do with his death."

Fi stayed silent.

"I loved that man. He was more of a father to me than my own dad, or the idiots my mother married. I spent the summers with him, here. It's part of the reason I took the job. How did it happen?"

"Heart attack."

"Thank goodness."

"Excuse me."

"I just thought…you talking to me…it was something else. So why are you asking me about dark magic?"

"Have you noticed anybody acting suspicious at the school?" It was a long shot, but there was no way she was going to tell a potential suspect they knew about necromancy.

"No, and it's something I do look for. Is there anything else?"

"The names. Of anyone who saw you Sunday morning or Saturday."

He scribbled something down on a piece of paper and handed it to her, but kept hold of the other end. "I heard it was you who recommended Diane for tutoring rather than incarceration."

Fi nodded.

"That was a wise decision. She's very talented."

"Thank you, and…I'm really sorry for your loss." Fi nodded again and left the room. As she walked back along the corridor, she heard a howl of grief from the classroom. She glanced at the short list in her hand. She'd check them out, but no one was that good an actor, were they?

Chapter 31

"Fiona! I thought I saw you in school," Diane called to Fi from further down the corridor.

"Hi." Fi forced a smile onto her face.

"What are you doing here?"

"Nothing. Just some MLO work."

"With Mr Lenoir? Are you consulting with him on a case? He's really good. He knows everything."

"Something like that." Fi frowned. Diane was curious and had a history of misusing magic. Maybe the teenager hadn't moved as far from the dark side as she let on. "So, what's he teaching you?"

"Mainly control." Diane rolled her eyes. "They've only unbound my magic enough to let me practice the theory. I can't wait to get all of it back again. Magic is awesome."

"Has he mentioned anything about…dark magic? Blood magic?"

"All the time. He won't stop going on about it. 'It's awful, it'll lead you astray, it's an easy route but not the right route'. As if I don't know that."

"When do you practice with him?"

"Twice a week, on Tuesdays and Thursdays. Good job it's not Fridays, that's when I go out with my friends."

"Your friends?"

"Yeah, Gill was really good about the whole necklace thing. She got that it was a mistake. I made her a luck charm to make up for it."

Gill must be a good friend if she forgave almost dying because of Diane's cursed necklace.

"We were out on Friday down the Witch's Brew," Diane carried on.

"Aren't you a bit young to be drinking?"

Diane winked at her. Oh to have that confidence.

"Well, I'd better go."

"Cool." And Diane scurried away to her next class.

Fi watched the teenager turn a corner before she headed back to find Cressida. A suspicion grew in her mind like one of the weeds in her sister's garden; what if tutor and pupil worked together?

Quentin teaching her and Diane practicing. She had prior history in misusing magic, and he had the knowledge. The anti-dark magic stance could all be an act. Definitely something to check out.

Chapter 32

Fi waved to Jack, Jeremy and Harris in their usual spots on the bench in front of the Witch's Brew pub. The green faced witch on the sign swung in the breeze. Fi frowned at it. She was never sure if it was cultural appropriation or stereotyping but it was good for business.

"Cheer up love, it might never happen," Jack – or maybe Jeremy – said.

"He's not worth it."

"He might be." Harris winked at her.

Idiots, said Cressida, walking past with her tail in the air.

Fi went inside, shaking her head at their antics. Some things never changed.

This was her last stop to check out Diane and Quentin's alibis. The school had confirmed they had been there all day – Quentin teaching and Diane attending classes – and, yes they had extra tutoring sessions on Tuesdays and Thursdays. And they both had alibis for Saturday before the party –

swimming lessons for Diane and pottery classes for Quentin. So that ruled them out for animating Mr Kite's body on the Saturday. Unless he'd been dead for a day when they'd done it.

Detective Ledd had been less than sympathetic when she'd called with an update, telling her to 'find another suspect and stop whining' followed by a lecture on going to see suspects without him. When she'd pointed out that he couldn't see anything thanks to the bandages, he had told her that his sight was almost back to normal thank you very much and hung up on her.

So here Fi was at the pub, checking if they were both here on Friday night.

Fi ordered a half pint of cider for herself, a pint for Mort who was on his way, a sparkling water for Cressida, and a plate of 'witches' fingers' or chipolatas with honey mustard dip before snagging a table as a couple stood up to leave.

When the barman came over with her order, she asked for a minute of his time while the food cooled.

"What can I do for you? We're a bit busy."

Fi could see. All the tables were packed. She recognised some locals, but most were tourists enjoying the strangely named food on the menu. "I just need to know if you saw either of these two last Friday." She held up a picture of Quentin for him to study.

"He was in here for sure. Often is on a Friday. Takes that booth in the corner, broods for a bit then plays darts with the lads."

"Quentin plays darts?"

"Sure. He's pretty good."

"And what about this girl?" Fi swiped to a photo of Diane.

"Not sure." He twisted the teatowel hung from his shoulder.

Fi sighed. "I'm with the Magical Liaison Office. I don't care if she's underage. I just need to know if she was here."

"Alright. A few of the teenagers come in on Fridays. What am I meant to do? Throw them out in the cold? But I only serve them soft drinks unless they've got ID. Is that all?"

Fi nodded and he headed back to the bar.

Pass me a sausage.

"They both have alibis, then. Is it wrong that I hoped they didn't come to the pub?"

Cressida didn't reply, but satisfied chomping came from her spot under the table.

Fi stood as Mort approached. "Hi you," he said.

"Hi yourself." She flung her arms around his neck and planted a kiss on his lips.

"What was that for?"

"An apology, for the other night. I shouldn't have blown you off."

"We should fall out more often. But it's OK to tell me you need some space, you know that?"

Fi smiled up and met his steady gaze. "I know, I've just got a lot on my mind."

"Any progress on the necromancer?"

She gave him a summary of her conversation with Quentin and his alibis. "So, now we're back to square one."

"Not quite square one."

"Oh?"

"I went to see Arawn. He's confident the book isn't in Omensford."

"How does that help?"

"Well, it means we can rule out anyone who lives here."

"But we don't have any other suspects!"

"Yet."

"You're optimistic."

"One of us has to be. Do you want to go now?"

Fi checked the time on her phone. "We've got time. Have a drink."

The garden centre would still be open in an hour, and then she could fulfil her promise.

Chapter 33

"Thanks for the lift."

"No problem, happy to help, you can't fit all those gnomes on the back of your vacuum cleaner."

"Plus if one of them fell out while I was flying…"

Best not to think about it

Mort winced. "Death on impact. What are we looking for?"

Fi clambered out of the four by four. "Just grab the most hideous gnomes you can find." She took one of the ginormous trollies at the entrance. In the way of all metal trolleys, it had one stuck wheel and listed to the left however she pushed it. Grunting with the effort of keeping it straight, she loaded it with all the brightly painted ugly gnomes out front. They headed inside and Fi insisted on going up and down all the aisles to find every last one.

These are hideous, Cressida said.

Mort grabbed a fat toad next to a giant toadstool. "Is this one?"

"I think that's just a genuine ceramic one."

"Are you sure? It's awful."

Fi considered it. "I think gnomes are human shaped. Are you a rock gnome?" she asked. The toad didn't move. Neither did any of the others.

A family passing in the opposite direction gave her a trio of funny looks.

Fi moved on. "Priapus said they had an in-built defence mechanism to turn to stone, I guess these are all in defence mode."

On the trolley, one gnome opened his eyes. "Did you say Priapus?"

Cressida hissed and jumped back.

"Yes."

"They do come alive!" Mort stared at the gnome.

"I told you. Yes, Priapus sent us to rescue you. This is a jail break."

"Thank you," he said out of the corner of his mouth.

"Is this one of you?" Mort asked.

"No. That's a statue of a toad."

"Told you."

Mort put down the offending amphibian.

"Are there any more of you?"

"Out back." The gnome returned to his rocklike state as a customer walked by. The woman eyed the trolley full of gnomes and raised her eyebrows but didn't say anything as she headed for the bedding plants.

Fi pushed the trolley to the back yard, only hitting two display stands on the way and they piled the remaining gnomes on top. The trolley became more unwieldy the more they loaded onto it and it took both of them to lug the flatbed to the tills.

The shopkeeper eyed the trolley as it bumped into the standing counter. "You a fan of gnomes, then?"

"Not really," Fi deadpanned. "Are these all of them?"

"Yep."

"You don't have any out back?"

"Don't you have enough?"

Fi smiled at him.

"Do you want me to check?"

"Please." She kept the bright smile on her face, and he bustled off with a look on his face that said he couldn't believe someone would want more gnomes. Fi could understand that.

He returned with two more. "That's your lot. You've cleaned us out."

He counted them and ran them up through the till before quoting a number so large that Fi could hear her bank account scream in protest.

"These are actually a magical species that I'm rescuing, so I'll take them for no charge."

"Pull the other one."

"Go on, move," Fi said to the gnomes. They stayed still.

"Are you wasting my time, miss?"

Fi coughed. "I don't suppose there's a bulk buy discount?"

"Tell you what, I'll knock ten per cent off," said the shop assistant, wanting to get the crazy gnome lady out of the garden centre.

The number was still enough to clear out her savings account.

"I'll get it," Mort offered.

"Nope. These are my gnomes, my problem. Maybe I can claim them back on expenses…" She paid the man and wheeled the trolley to the car. "And you lot were no help."

The gnomes stayed in their rock forms. Fi and Mort stopped the trolley just before it hit his car and loaded them into the boot, and the back seat, and the footwells.

"They won't all fit."

"They're stone. Just pile them on top of each other. They won't mind as long as they stay in this form." Fi pushed the remainder in and took the trolley back, abandoning it in the allocated space.

Mort drove them to Agatha's and they unloaded the gnomes into her garden, covering every inch of green lawn with the heavy creatures.

"Welcome gnome."

"Why aren't they coming alive?" asked Mort.

Priapus waddled over and surveyed the gnomes. "Don't worry. We're nocturnal. What's this?" He kicked a small gnome in an orange mankini. "This isn't one of my people."

It looks just as awful as the others.

"Easy mistake to make," Fi said.

He sniffed. "Well, thank you for rescuing everyone. We owe you a great debt. I pledge myself to your service until I can return the debt." With that, he turned back to his own stone form.

"Hold on, I don't want your service." Too late. Fi's protest fell on stone ears.

"Are you alright with this many gnomes, Aggy?"

"Of course, poor dears. I'm happy to help. They can stay as long as they need. Do you two want to stay for dinner?"

"Actually, I thought we could go back to Mort's and chill."

"Really?" Mort sounded surprised.

"Yeah. I'm trying this new thing where I stop pushing away the people I love."

Agatha squealed and Fi glared at her.

"But I just want to watch some bad TV and eat some takeaway. No long conversations," Fi added, setting her boundaries.

"Noted. Any other requests?" Mort asked with a twinkle in his dark eyes.

Fi's mouth curved up. "Maybe I'll think of something…"

Chapter 34

The next morning, Fi strolled home, content with the world. It was still too early in the morning, but Mort had been called out to an out of hours doctor emergency and she hadn't wanted to stay in the house with his dad, so she'd decided to do the walk of shame home instead, still wearing yesterday's clothes. Despite the early hour, she was happy. Last night had been fun – Mort hadn't even mentioned proposing – and she was still on a high from seeing the rescued rock gnomes in Agatha's garden. That birthday present had gone even better than she'd dreamed. If only her case could go that smoothly.

Fi dug her hands into the pockets of her faded baggy jeans and toyed with her keyring. Her fingers traced the luck charm Diane had given her. How did that thing work anyway? She pulled it out and stared at it.

What are you doing? Cressida asked as she trotted at Fi's ankles.

"Trying to get some luck."

Superstitious nonsense. You make your own luck.

"That's rich, you're always banging on about superstitious stuff."

Traditions, Fiona. That's different.

Fi snorted and stuffed the keys back into her pocket. She looked around and the old Tudor building that housed the town's small museum caught her eye. The sign said 'open' despite the early hour and a strange desire to go inside gripped Fi. She decided to go with it, maybe that was how the luck charm worked. "I didn't know the museum was open today. Shall we go in? Look at some traditions?"

Are you feeling quite alright? You don't normally want to educate yourself.

Fi shrugged. Something about the small building drew her to it today. Maybe it was her good mood, maybe it was the luck charm, maybe it was the sign outside that promised a discount in the coffee shop with all tickets.

She climbed the steps and entered a cluttered room that was the town's museum.

"Welcome, welcome," a wizened old man stood from his stool.

"Mr Bombil, you still work here?"

"Not so much work as having a vocation to care for our town's treasures. The good and the bad."

Fi raised an eyebrow.

"Do you want a tour?" He leaned forward, eager to offer to educate her.

"Yes, please."

Mr Bombil bimbled around the room, which was no bigger than the kitchen at her mothers Bed & Breakfast and pointed out interesting artefacts; the town charter, a copy of the certificate of designation that made Omensford a protected magical area, an iron age sword found in one of the fields nearby, photos of the town from bygone years and so on. There were some magical items too, although nothing too dangerous; simple family grimoires and old potion bottles. Cressida lingered over the bottles with fondness.

Just like Goody used to have.

Fi patted her on the head. It was rare for Cressida to mention her former witch, a formidable potion mistress and Chair of the Magewell branch of the Witches', Wizards' and Warlocks' Institute who had been murdered a couple of years ago.

They continued on and Fi stopped in front of a cabinet holding a wicked looking spell book with a card next to it that purported that the book could raise the dead. This couldn't be linked to the necromancer, that would be too easy.

"What's this?"

"Ah yes, our Book of the Dead. A replica of course. We couldn't risk showing the real thing. It's probably a hoax, but just in case, the real one is in our basement."

"Can I see it?"

"Ah, a history buff. I shouldn't really."

"It would help with my investigation." Fi flashed her Magical Liaison Office ID and Mr Bombil drew himself upright with a gleam in his eye.

"Well, if I can help the authorities…" He locked up and led the way downstairs to the basement where he passed piles of cardboard boxes with labels like; 'old phone books' and 'Omensford magazine issues 121-246'.

Mr Bombil stopped in front of a set of metal shelves and frowned. "It should be here, somewhere…maybe the cleaner moved it." He searched the shelves, moving boxes out of the way then stepped back. "It's not here. The book is gone."

"Do you have any digital copies of what's inside it?"

"Goodness me, no. I've prioritised digitising our photos, not old books. Good thing it can't really raise the dead, hey?" He laughed. "And good thing you're here, I can report it stolen."

Chapter 35

I HAVE BEEN WAITING FOR YOU TO RETURN.

Fi jumped as she almost walked straight into Arawn's tall avatar in the B&B's cosy kitchen.

So this is the god who dragged you through a portal without me. Cressida raised her hackles and hissed.

"Easy, Cressida." Fi put her hand over her eyes. "Why don't you go wait by the fire?"

And leave you with him?

"Please, for me?"

Hmmph. Cressida stalked off and curled up by the aga, with both eyes fixed on the God of Death.

"Sorry about that, I had a gnome problem to deal with and I almost found the book."

He raised one perfect eyebrow. BUT YOU DID NOT. It wasn't a question.

"What do you know?"

I HAVE DISCOVERED THE LOCATION OF THE BOOK.

"Brilliant. So, you can go and get it and–"

I CANNOT INTERVENE IN THIS. IT IS TOO MORTAL.

"O…K…"

THIS IS ALL THE ASSISTANCE I CAN GIVE YOU. I DO NOT KNOW IF THE NECROMANCER WILL BE WITH THE BOOK.

He handed over a piece of paper with the address printed on it.

"Thank you. I'll check it out."

LIVES DEPEND ON YOU. NOW I MUST RETURN TO MY REALM, THE BARRIERS WEAKEN FURTHER.

He raised his hand and a sucking portal appeared, the colour of the night sky. He stepped through and disappeared. Fi turned the paper over and looked at the font. It was exactly the sort of script she'd expect the God of Death to have. She looked up the address. A large, detached house about five miles away. Isolated. She zoomed out on the map view. And next to a church with a graveyard. The perfect place for a necromancer to practice. A shiver ran up her spine and goosepimples rose on her arm despite the warmth of the kitchen.

Her mother entered via the door. "Where's Aaron? Such a sweet man, very thoughtful, made his own bed."

"He had to go."

She sniffed. "Good job he paid in advance then." Her mum held out a small leather pouch and emptied the gold coins onto the table. "Not many people pay in antique coins. I'm sure this is worth more than the usual rate, I expect he'll want a refund."

"No?"

"Who was he?"

"What do you mean?"

"You can't keep things from me, child." She tapped her cane on the ground to emphasise her point.

Fi sighed. "He was the God of Death, checking up on the case."

"I knew it. The house decorated his room to look like some sort of castle…"

Fi shrugged. "No idea what his style is. At least it wasn't a sex swing."

They both shuddered at the memory of the quiet couple who had turned out to be nymphomaniacs. The house catered for any taste, including sex dungeon apparently.

"Don't be vulgar." Her mother marched to the oven, her walking stick clacking on the flagstone floor. "At least he won't want a refund, gods don't usually care about that sort of thing." Nell pocketed the coins.

"How many gods have you had stay here?" Fi asked.

"I suppose his breakfast will go to waste now."

"Ah-ah, I'll take it." Fi swooped in with a plate before her mother could bin the tantalising full English and made herself a bacon and mushroom sandwich.

What about me? Cressida asked from her spot by the aga style cooker.

Fi chucked her a sausage and sat down at the table, watching her mum tidy up, still clutching the cane in her hand.

Fi coughed. "Mum…"

"Yes?"

"I was round this house the other day and they had this cool chair…"

"Oh?"

"Yeah, it was one where it helped whoever sat on it to stand."

"Really." The temperature in the room dropped several degrees.

Fi swallowed and pressed on. "Yeah. I thought it might be good to get one. For the house."

Cressida choked on her sausage.

"And why would that be?" The shadows in the corners of the room darkened.

"Well, you know, you need a walking stick and you're getting on a bit."

"How old do you think I am, Fiona Blair?" Her mother's eyes glittered hard as sapphires as she stared down her daughter.

Fi looked away.

It's a trick question. Don't answer.

Fi shot a look at her familiar. She wasn't that dense. She coughed again. "I just thought…"

"The day when I need any sort of living aid is a long way away and don't you forget it."

"But, the stick."

Her mother's eyes blazed and the stick disintegrated into a pile of dust on the floor. The metal cat that topped the cane hit the stone with a clang. "Happy now? You can clean that up." With that, she swept out of the room.

Well done.

Fi glared at the small wyrm.

No, I mean it. Really tactful.

"Oh, shut up." She got up, binned the cat shaped topper, and used her state-of-the-art vacuum cleaner to hoover up the remains of the cane.

Chapter 36

Fi looked down at her phone. She'd sent several apology texts to her mother and had no reply. Her fingers hovered over the screen. Was seven texts too many? Probably not. She typed out another, but before she could press send, the phone rang. Unknown number.

"Hello?"

"Fiona? It's Robbie, the coroner. I've got Larry on the line too."

"Get on with it," Larry's voice came over the speaker.

"I've got an ID on the body from the curryhouse. Orlando Heap. Lived in Magewell. Eighty-nine years old. Lived in an assisted living facility just off the high street."

"Good work, Robbie."

"That's not all, I've got a C.O.D too."

"C.O.D?" Fi asked.

"Cause of death." Of course. Stupid of Fi not to know that given how many true crime podcasts she'd listened to over the years. Mentally kicking herself, Fi tuned back in to Robbie's summary. "Overdose of painkillers. Not a bad way to go, all things considered."

"Suicide?"

"Can't say for sure but he had soup in his stomach too and the painkillers were all mixed in along with sleeping pills. My best guess is someone dissolved the medication in the meal."

"Poison then," Fi said.

"Looks that way. But we can't rule out him taking the medication himself. Either way, there was no medical reason why he should have been up and about that evening. He'd been dead for at least twenty-four hours."

"Definitely magic then." The detective sighed. "Fiona, any leads?"

Fi took the scrap of paper from her pocket. "Maybe…"

"Care to share?"

She frowned. Care. That was a possible link. Better to check out actual evidence first rather than go on a whim and trust a god. Besides, he didn't know who the necromancer was. Fi decided to trust her gut. They needed the necromancer, not just the book. "Who helped him at this assisted living facility?"

"What are you thinking?" the detective asked.

"I'm wondering if there's a link with his care company?"

"Good thinking." Fi could hear the clicking of the detective's loud, one-fingered typing through the phone. She winced at the mistreatment of the keyboard. "The facility is run by Open Homes…but, looks like there's a contract with Cotswolds Help and Care." A rustle of paper told Fi that he was checking his notebook. "That's the company Kite's cleaner works for. Good instincts. Fancy coming with me to talk to the owner?"

"Pick me up on the way?"

~

An hour later, the detective pulled up outside an industrial estate on the outskirts of Cirencester. In contrast to the olde world charm of the ancient roman town, the industrial estate was a squat set of single storey buildings that looked like they had been discarded from the blandest buildings town planning had ever conceived.

Despite the bright sunshine, a depth of despair hovered over the grey buildings. Peeling paint and dirty windows added to the depressing look and the scent of chemicals mixed with exhaust fumes sat perfectly with the décor.

"Is this where hope goes to die?"

"Didn't you used to work in IT?"

"Yeah, but…" Fi stopped. Answering calls from people who understood nothing about how computers work had been pretty depressing. Getting fired had been worse though. She followed the detective through an open door that had Cotswolds Help and Care painted over it in large letters that had once been bright, but a combination of the weather and the general sucking lethargy of the place had conspired to mute any but the palest shades of colour.

"Mrs Brittle?" The detective addressed a small woman with her hair scraped back so tightly over her head that Fi could see the shape of her skull. He showed her his ID and she gave a small smile.

"Detective Ledd. A pleasure. Please. Call me Simone." The woman spoke in clipped sentences, as if each word was an effort to get out. She eyed Fiona.

"Fiona Blair. Magical Liaison Office." Fi shook the limp hand that Simone proffered. It was cool and calloused.

"And you own the Cotswolds Help and Care?"

"Yes. Twenty years of care in the community." Fi thought there might have been a tinge of pride in her voice, but it was hard to be sure with such short bursts of speech.

"Two of your clients have died in the past week."

"A shame. But it happens. We care for people who are not well, Detective. Clients die." She shrugged.

"What puzzles me is why no one on your team reported it?"

Simone quirked her head so suddenly that Fi was afraid her neck might snap. "I don't understand."

"Your team cares for these people. They are there regularly and yet no one reported the deaths."

"There is a procedure to follow in these situations. My team are all briefed to follow it. If they didn't report it, it's because no one was there."

"I'll need to see the schedules for Misters Kite and Heap."

Simone turned to a computer and pulled the schedules up on screen before printing them out. "Here. My team sticks to the same weekly schedule. Makes it easier for them to plan their lives outside of work."

Detective Ledd scanned the sheet before passing it to Fi. She looked down the names.

"Not full-time care, then?"

"No. Live-in carers are a special request. Most people tend to avoid it unless there's no alternative. Neither Mr Kite nor Mr Heap had live-in carers, just people who helped out with the cleaning, made sure they took medication, that sort of thing."

"This is the same rota every week?" Fi asked.

Simone's eyes darted to her. "Yes."

"What about holidays?"

"We normally get in agency workers to cover holidays. We have a few regulars."

"Janine was on holiday last week…what about…" Fi found the name of Heap's carer, "…Clare."

Simone tapped on the keyboard again. "Yes. Janine was off last week and Clare was away this week."

"Who covered for them?"

"One of our agency workers. From Sunflower Agency. Give me a moment…Harriet Still."

Fi's eyes widened. Detective Ledd noticed and pursed his fat lips. "The name means something to you."

"Yes. She works with my sister. And I think I know where she is." Fi pulled the scrap of paper with the address on it from her pocket.

Chapter 37

"You're sure it's here?" Detective Ledd asked, holding a pair of binoculars up to his eyes.

Doesn't he trust you?

"That's the lead I've got." Fi didn't tell him that the God of Death had given it to her. There was only so much supernatural that the detective could take and somehow, she didn't think gods were on that list.

Fi searched for something else to talk about. "How's it going with the warlock? Miranda?"

"None of your business."

"That bad, huh?"

"She couldn't make it for the weekend, that's all."

"What's her last name?" Fi pulled out her phone.

The detective's eyes narrowed with suspicion. "Why?"

"I can look her up, check she's doing what she's told you."

You can share another pearl of wisdom with my followers too; don't interrupt your afternoon nap for a stakeout.

"You insisted on coming," Fi told her familiar.

I can't trust you not to disappear through portals without me.

The detective tsked. "I trust Miranda completely." There was a long pause. "Besides, I already checked."

"Hah!"

Check my follower count.

"You're obsessed."

"Looking at someone's social media account does not mean you're obsessed," Detective Ledd said, slamming his hand on the steering wheel.

"Not you, Cressida, oh never mind."

Mort's black four by four pulled up behind them and he got out. Fi swallowed as she took in the sword at his side. It was sharp enough to cut through anything, but whenever he wore it, he changed. He stood straighter, his cheeks hollowed, he grew taller, and he gave off a power that Fi couldn't place. The embodiment of death's servant. He adjusted the sword and got into the car.

"This is it?"

Fi nodded. "Can you sense anything?"

His face softened for a second. "Like what?"

"Death stuff."

"Death stuff?"

Death stuff? Cressida repeated. *Really? That's the best you can come up with?*

"Yeah, like anyone using magic."

"That's your area, not mine."

Fi closed her eyes and concentrated. She reached out a hand to her familiar and combined their energies to expand her senses over the overgrown lawn towards the towering gothic house. Was that something moving in the garden? Fi shook her head. "No. I'm too far away. We'll have to get closer."

She made to open the car door, but the detective stopped her. "I don't like this."

"We have to check it out."

"We should get a team in place."

"What if she's not in there? And what are a team going to do against a necromancer?"

He didn't have a response to that.

"Look, why don't me and Mort go and have a closer look. We'll be stealthy."

"Stealthy?"

"Yeah, and if she sees us, I'll just say we were on a walk."

"With a sword?"

Fi looked at Mort. He sighed and the weapon disappeared from his side.

"I think I should come with you," Larry insisted.

"How can we say we're on a couple's walk if there's three of us?"

Larry crossed his arms and sank back in his seat. "Fine. But I don't like it. And first sign of trouble, you get out of there."

"We'll be back before you know it." Fi scooped Cressida up and shut the door gently behind her.

She signalled to Mort and they walked past the house and looped around the walled garden.

"Arawn was sure the book is in here?"

Fi nodded, her mouth dry. Mort looked around. "Shall I give you a boost?"

Fi looked up at the wall. It was about three inches above her head and the crumbling brickwork bowed out in a bulge that suggested it had seen better days. She shook her head. "There'll be a gate."

They followed the wall and Fi smirked when she saw the battered wooden gate. "Told you."

Cressida hopped down and wriggled under a gap beneath the gate.

All clear.

She relayed the message to Mort before trying the ringed iron handle.

Locked.

It was his turn to smirk. "How about that boost?"

Fi sighed and placed her trainer into his cupped hand, launching herself to the top of the wall. Dust fell from the angled capped brick on top, smearing her baggy jeans with white powder, but the wall didn't shift under her weight so she took that as a win. She swung her legs up and over and jumped down into a bush.

"Ouch."

"What's wrong?" Mort whispered from the top of the wall.

"Rose bush."

Mort shuffled along the wall, his clothes rustling against the brick before landing with a dull thud on the grass next to the roses.

"Why did you jump into a rose bush?"

Fi turned her head and tugged at the thorns that held her captive. "I didn't know it was a bloody rose bush, did I? You could have warned me, Cress."

I got distracted. You know me, too obsessed with my followers.

Darn touchy familiars.

Mort gave a low chuckle and grasped her hand. "On the count of three. One, two…" He pulled, wrenching her from the bush. Fi grimaced in pain as the thorns scraped her skin and she heard the tear of fabric as they released her.

"You went on two."

He shrugged. "Sorry, doctor habit."

Fi shook her head and inspected her grazes. Nothing major. She swore.

"What's wrong?" Mort moved closer and ran his hands down her arms, searching for injuries.

"My favourite t-shirt. It's ruined." She held up the purple fabric, now spotted with tiny tears.

Is that all?

Fi sighed. Mort lifted one eyebrow. "It's alright for you, Cressida. You don't wear clothes."

The wyrm gave a snotty hmmph and ran across the lawn in a flash of gold. Fi and Mort exchanged a look and they raced across the garden in an awkward half crouch until they were right outside the house.

Something rustled in the border nearby. Fi whipped her head round but couldn't see anything. Probably a bird or something natural like that.

Fi crouched behind a bushy shrub and winced as a spiky branch scraped her side. Why were all plants against her? She put one hand on the smooth stone of the windowsill and peeked in. There was Hetty, talking to a chest freezer.

Fi scowled. It didn't make sense – how could a necromancer have a name like Hetty? Shouldn't their name be more menacing? Fi's phone rang, breaking through her scattered thoughts. Hetty turned, a frown creasing her face.

Fi swore and answered, keeping her voice to a whisper.

"Aggy? I can't talk–"

"Have you found anywhere for them to stay?"

"I thought you were happy to have them at yours?"

"That was before they tried to eat Cluck and Kylo."

"Not Kylo Hen!" Kylo was Fi's favourite chicken. Privately, Fi thought the world would be better off without Cluck Norris – Agatha's evil rooster – in it.

"And they've ruined my veg patch. How am I supposed to compete in any of the best in shows without any produce?"

"Come on, Aggy, you can grow anything."

"I want them gone."

"They've only been there one night."

"I mean it, Fiona."

Fi winced. Her sister had used her full name. This was serious. "I'll find somewhere."

"Good. And apologise to Mum. I don't know what you said but she's started trying to prove she can do everything by herself. I caught her on her broomstick cleaning out the gutters." Her sister hung up.

Fi sighed. Another problem to add to her list. Right after stopping a necromancer. She risked another look through the window. Hetty had gone.

<h1 style="text-align:center">Chapter 38</h1>

Fi looked around, the branches of the shrub snagging her dishevelled hair. Maybe Hetty had just gone somewhere else in the house.

"Hello?" A bright voice sounded from the front door. Fi cursed under her breath – her phone had given them away. What to do? Stay put and hope for the best, or leg it over the garden? Fi met Mort's gaze and made her decision.

She stepped out from the shrubbery and walked around to meet Hetty. Behind her, Mort groaned and there was a rustle of leaves as he came to her side.

"Hi there," Fi said with a wave as she aimed for casual nonchalance.

"Fiona. What a pleasant surprise. What are you doing here?"

"Just out for a walk."

"And do you make it a habit to trespass on your walks?"

Fi gave a laugh that aimed for breezy but came across as brittle. "My wyrm ran under the gate so I followed. You know how pets can be."

Cressida sauntered up to Fi and rubbed her head on Fi's leg. *That was the best you could come up with?*

"You should have her on a lead." Hetty's smile didn't make it to her eyes.

"Yes, well, we'll just be on our way. Lovely house."

"Oh, you must come in for a cup of tea."

"We should be getting on…"

"I insist. I haven't had a chance to meet your boyfriend properly and Agatha talks about you two all the time in the staff room."

Fi's fists clenched but she couldn't see a way out. She forced a smile. "Of course."

The old house loomed above them, its corners peaked with turrets and its stone walls greyed with time and covered by dark ivy that threatened to choke off the entire right side of the building. Fi swallowed as she followed Hetty inside, feeling like it was the sort of place that could feature in a horror film – the type of house no one escaped from.

She reached down and gripped Mort's hand in hers, and he squeezed back, the warmth of his palm lending her courage.

Inside, the musty scent of decay filled her nostrils. She glanced at Cressida, who flicked her tongue out.

I can smell mould and bleach, and rotting flesh.

Fi reached out with her magic, probing ahead but she couldn't sense anything. Hetty led them to a kitchen where she put the kettle on and rooted around in a cupboard for mugs. A layer of dust covered the chairs, as if the house hadn't been lived in for a long time. Hetty flicked a tea towel at them and gestured for them to sit. Fi eased onto the chair, sitting on the edge and screwing up her face as the dust joined the smear of white brick powder on her jeans. A bump sounded in the house.

"Someone else here?"

"Hmmm? Oh, no. The house makes noises sometimes, that's all. Let me see, I've got…tea…or coffee. No milk though."

Strange that she had to look to see what drinks she had in the cupboard, thought Fi as she looked around. The entire kitchen had a thick layer of dust around it, as if no one lived here. The only thing that looked clean was the chest freezer.

"Coffee, please. Have you lived here long?"

"Not really, I've…inherited the place."

The bumping noise sounded again, closer this time, followed by a scraping. Fi's head swivelled. "There's something here."

"Don't be silly." Hetty placed two cups of coffee on the table. Fi lifted her cup, noting the ring it had made in the dust and took a sip. "Now, tell me, how did you two meet?"

Mort took up the small talk with ease and he relayed the story of how they'd first met at the Halloween Fete. Fi pushed away the memories of her first encounter with murder and its aftermath that had culminated in her vaporising the killer. Guilt wouldn't help her now. Instead, she focused on her training and pushed her magic into the familiar link between herself and Cressida. It took away the brute force of her power and lent her a subtlety that she didn't possess on her own.

Once her magic was dampened, she reached out, sensing for other magic in the house. Her power brushed against something outside the door. Something large that was coated with that same cold, dark feeling she had sensed on Mr Kite's animated corpse.

Fi shuddered and her eyes snapped open. "There's something in the hall."

"Nonsense. Let me go and see." Hetty gave a strained smile and headed into the hall. Fi leaned back to get a view of the hallway, but Hetty's poufy dress blocked her view and with a swish of her hips, the door shut behind her.

"It's definitely her."

Mort nodded and his sword appeared in his hand, ready for danger. Fi got to her feet, ignoring the tickle in her throat and pushed the door open. Hetty was halfway down the hall, shoving someone backwards. Fi squinted in the gloomy light and found the switch. She pressed it and the electric light flared on, illuminating the greyed skin and decomposing flesh of another animated corpse.

Hetty turned, her lips pressed into a furious line. "You weren't meant to see him."

"Who is he?"

She sighed. "He died naturally. That was when I got the idea. It's tricky to animate a corpse, especially a human, so complicated, but I managed it with Denzel. Of course, you can see that he's been here a while and he's not exactly the brightest tool in the shed." Hetty prodded the zombie in the chest to emphasise her point. Denzel didn't even blink, just stared ahead with misty eyes. "That's where I got the idea, then it was just a case of refining it with others."

"Why?"

"Do you know how strong muscle memory is? It's quite easy for people to go into their routines, and corpses aren't constrained by the pain people felt in life. Mr Kite was quite nimble, decided to go down the shops, which I'll admit was a bit of a surprise as he hadn't left the house in over a year, but I couldn't pass up the opportunity once I found him waiting for me. Dead in a chair, poor man. But he had his uses in the end."

"Why do you need zombies?" Fi asked, leaning forward.

"Zombies? No, no. Not zombies. They're people."

"They're dead."

Hetty's lips pressed together again. "I prefer to think of them as vitally challenged. And if I can stop that, if I can get them back to life, I can have him back."

A jigsaw piece slotted together in Fi's head. "Your son."

Tears filled Hetty's eyes, and she nodded, unable to speak.

"Hetty, it doesn't work like that. I'm sorry, but there are lines and death is one of them. Your son can't live again," Mort said.

"That's not true. Look at Denzel."

"He's not exactly living though, is he?" Fi said.

"I just need more time. Each time, they do more than before. It's only a matter of time before I get it right. I just need more practice.

"Why don't we sit down and talk and you can give me the book and we'll sort this out."

Hetty's gaze darted to the kitchen door for a second before she looked Fi right in the eyes. "The thing about animating corpses is that it's quite simple to have them under my control. The trick is getting them to have their own freedom."

Fi took a step backwards. A bolt of fear racked through her at the matter-of-fact way Hetty spoke.

"So I could say to Denzel to attack. And he would."

"Hetty…" Fi took another step away.

The necromancer in a summery dress laughed as she walked past them to the kitchen and Fi let out a sigh of relief. She was going to come quietly after all.

At the doorway, Hetty paused and looked over her shoulder. "Denzel. Get rid of them."

Chapter 39

The zombie lurched at Fi, taking a large shuffling step towards her. She raised her hands, her magic whirling around her fingers, but Mort shoved Fi to the side and stepped in front of her, sword raised. He was a trained fighter. Death's servant. He could handle a lurching undead zombie.

Fi scrambled backwards into the kitchen and turned to face Hetty. The necromancer stood next to the open freezer, a large book in her hands. It was bound in pale leather with a raised face embossed on it. Fi gagged as she realised that it wasn't embossing, it was a dried human face, stretched to cover the book's bindings and sewn to other scraps of flesh. The book was so much worse than the copy in the museum.

Fi had seen books bound in human leather in her mother's library, but nothing like this. Waves of evil magic came off it in invisible bursts.

Hetty licked her finger and turned a page. "I'm so close. The last few have gone back to their usual routines, a bit sluggish to be sure, but they mimic the living."

"Mimic. That's all they're doing. They're not alive."

"I know that." She pushed her hands through her blonde hair. "Don't you think I know that? But I'd give anything to see him walk through the door again, talk to me again, hold me."

"Who?"

"Liam. My baby boy. I'm so close. I just need more practice to get the spell right."

"We can't allow that, Hetty."

She pursed her lips and shook her head. The hem of her flowery dress bounced around her knees. "Unacceptable." She muttered some words and Fi called her power to her hands, ready to shock the necromancer.

The door burst open.

Corpses in various states of disgusting decay shambled into the room.

Fi's gaze drifted to the window. Of course. They were right next to a cemetery. Fi swore. Hetty had an army here.

"Attack," she said.

Watch out! Cressida shouted in her mind.

Fi shot a bolt of electricity at one of them and it veered to one side but kept coming. She launched more and more of her power at the undead bodies but they ignored her magic, caught up by the necromancy that powered them.

Cressida snapped at the closest ankle and gagged. *This is the most disgusting thing I've had in my mouth. And I tried those vegan sausages your sister bought.*

Behind her, Hetty's muttering continued as she summoned more and more of the creatures to do her bidding.

A cold hand gripped her wrist and pulled her towards it. Fi wrenched her hand out of its weak grasp and the hand came away, still attached to her wrist. She stared down at it in shock and punched out at the decomposing head far too close to her for comfort. The skin exploded around her fist like it was dust and she gagged as she inhaled some of the powdery mist. How old were these corpses?

She wasn't strong, but the impact shook the head from its spine and the creature collapsed to the ground. "Go for the head!" Fi shouted to Mort, the words coming out in a choked garble around her coughing fit as she tried to spit out the skin dust she'd breathed in.

Mort appeared at her side, sword in hand. "Way ahead of you." With a twirl of his wrist, he slashed across the next zombie, decapitating it in a practised motion.

Fi grabbed a chair and smashed it against the closest zombie, shattering the wooden chair to pieces and sending dust flying. Fi sneezed. The green-skinned creature kept coming, arms outstretched in a classic horror movie pose. Fi gripped the chair leg still in her hand and shoved it into the zombie's open mouth, covering her nose as she sneezed over and over.

More zombies piled through the door. Mort pulled her up onto the table and she kicked out at one that was practically a skeleton, with only the barest scraps of flesh still clinging to its yellowed bones.

Through her sneezing fit, she stared at the book in Hetty's hands. The source of all the necromancer's power. She took aim and felt something grasp her ankle. It pulled and she slammed into the table. Fi kicked free and scrambled to the centre of the table. She held up her hand and blasted the book with a bolt of electricity. The tome exploded and charred pages floated to the ground, the knowledge lost.

Hetty gaped. "You destroyed it."

Fi pushed herself up. "Yep. That's the end of it. Now, come with us and I'll put in a good word with the Magical Liaison Office…"

The necromancer laughed. It started low and mounted to a high-pitched uncontrollable giggle that bounced around the room. "You think destroying the book can stop me."

"Well…yes…you don't have the spells anymore."

Oh no…

"You're more stupid than you look." Hetty pulled out her phone and began reading from the screen.

Fi's mouth dropped. The necromancer had taken pictures of the pages. Bloody modern technology.

Chapter 40

But Fi could deal with technology. She gathered her electrical magic to her and let loose, allowing herself to lose control and get caught up in the exhilaration of letting her power flood through her. She directed her magic at the necromancer, shorting out the phone with an anticlimactic fizz.

"You destroyed it!" Hetty stabbed at the screen with her index finger. Her chest heaved. "Why did you do that, you idiot? You've ruined everything."

"Why aren't the zombies stopping?"

"You don't even understand what you've done, do you? You haven't broken my link with them." Hetty gave a nasty smile. "I ordered them to do something. They won't stop until it's done. And I need to get my back-up data." With a sing-song order of "Get them," Hetty shimmied through the crowd of corpses she'd raised to the chest freezer.

Bloody cloud data back-ups. All Fi had done was destroy a phone.

Fi kicked out again as Mort swiped with his sword, taking out another of the necromancer's minions. She cried out as one of the creatures sank its teeth into her calf. Now she was going to turn into a zombie too. Or was that just in films?

Beside her, zombies shuffled onto the table, surrounding Mort. Her chest felt like it was made of lead. She couldn't lose him. She might not want to marry him, but she loved him. She pulled at the nearest one, but couldn't move its weighty body. And really, was marriage so bad?

She wasn't going to lose Mort. Giving up on moving the zombies, she changed tactic and leapt from the table to the kitchen, ducking past groping hands.

Something hard slammed into her ankle. "Watch where you're going!" a voice like gravel shouted up at her.

"Priapus? What are you doing here?" Fi ducked to avoid a zombie's grasp.

"Helping you. Like I pledged. Looks like you've got a situation here. Duck!" He chopped off a zombie's foot, laughed like a maniac as it fell to the floor, then proceeded to ram his axe into its head.

"But how did you–?"

"Less talking, more chopping." Priapus hacked at another of the undead creatures with gusto.

Fi stared at him until a zombie grabbed her shoulder and hauled her back into the fray.

What are you doing?

Fi ignored her familiar and scrabbled around in the drawers until she found a meat cleaver and a large kitchen knife. She held them up, screamed and hacked at the nearest monster. It fell to the ground as she destroyed its skull. Panting and with a mad gleam in her eye, she aimed for the next one.

Get the necromancer, you idiot.

Cressida's words cut through the fog of anger and pain that drove her. Yes. The necromancer. Where was she? Fi took in the empty chest freezer, its lid flung open. She'd gone. Fi reached out with her power, trying to sense the crackle of electricity that flowed through every living thing. A hand grabbed her and she lost focus.

"Er, I'm a bit busy now, Cressida." Fi chopped at the grasping hand then stabbed the zombie in the eye, trying not to think about her actions. It was like a videogame, that's all. A graphic videogame. And it wasn't like she could kill something that was already dead…could she?

A rasping hand around her neck pulled her out of her spiralling thoughts and she hacked at the new attacker, panting hard at the exertion.

Fine, I'll do it myself.

From the hallway came a loud scream followed by a growl and a thud.

"Cressida!"

Mort slashed his way through the diminishing horde and reached her side. Only three zombies left. She held up her hand and blasted one in the face with a bolt of electricity. Her power might not work in a subtle way, but scorching its skull counted for something. It lurched towards her for a millisecond before it fell to the ground, the remains of its brain fried. Mort disposed of the other two and they raced into the hallway.

Chapter 41

Hetty leant against the wall, kicking out at Cressida who darted at her feet, teeth bared. A tall, blonde man loomed to her side. He was dressed in a rugby kit and stared blankly across the room.

"Get back!"

"Cressida, what are you doing?"

What does it look like I'm doing. I'm apprehending the necromancer.

The golden wyrm shot a look at Fi as she dashed in again and yelped as Hetty's foot connected with her side.

"Get away from my familiar!" Fi squared her shoulders and took a step towards the woman. Cressida huddled next to the stairs and Fi reached out through the familiar bond to sense her injuries. Anger, pain and fear shot across the bond. Fi sent soothing thoughts to her wyrm and moved to be close to her.

"Liam! Help me!"

The golden-haired corpse lunged forward stiffly, shifting in front of his mother. Fi jerked to a halt. The zombie towered over six foot with the broad shoulders and thick legs of a rugby player. She swallowed. No chance of pushing through.

Mort stepped to her side and pushed her behind him. The zombie punched out, his ham sized fist connecting hard with the side of Mort's head. The punch shoved Mort against Fi and she grunted at the impact.

Going by instinct, she loosed electricity at the creature. It did nothing. She swore.

Electricity doesn't work on them, they're controlled by magic. You'll wear yourself out if you try to zap them all with lightning level power. Cressida panted out laboured breaths.

"You're not helping," Fi said through gritted teeth. She knew electricity didn't work, but she didn't have anything else. "Get out of here, get to safety."

The zombie hit Mort again, sending a shockwave through the dazed doctor's body. Fi sidestepped out from behind her boyfriend and shoved the huge corpse as hard as she could. He ignored her hits. Fi let out a roar of frustration and pummelled him again. She couldn't move him. Hitting the cold body was like punching a frozen chunk of meat.

But her efforts drew his attention. He turned milky eyes to her and opened his mouth. Fi stopped. He looked…sad. Somewhere in his murky spelled consciousness, did he realise that he was an unnatural being and long for freedom from the undead?

He reached for her, and she barely ducked in time, too consumed with her sympathy for the creature. Now was not a good time to get in touch with her emotions. The zombie grabbed her hair and pulled, yanking her up. Fi screamed and kicked out. His other hand closed around her and Fi clawed at it.

A flash of gold darted past. Not aiming for the zombie, but for the necromancer. Hetty. Some part of her foggy brain shouted at Fi that it needed oxygen. Fi kicked free, leaving a chunk of her white hair in the zombie's hand.

Hetty lashed out with a foot and a wave of pain shot through Cressida, spiking Fi through the familiar bond. Of course. The necromancer. Take her out and it would all stop.

"This is for you, Cressida." No one hurt Fi's familiar and got away with it.

Fi gathered her power and aimed a bolt of electricity at Hetty. She wasn't subtle, but she stopped short of lethal force. Hetty collapsed to the ground with a sob.

"Atta girl," came Priapus' voice from the doorway.

At the exact moment that Fi launched her electricity, Mort lunged at the zombie son and decapitated him with a swift cut of his sword. The zombie fell to the floor with a thud and a separate, smaller thud as his head rolled across the floorboards.

"No, no, no, no. Not again. He can't be dead again." Hetty crawled over to her son's body and cradled it, warm tears falling on his cold body. "Not my boy, not my darling boy."

Fi looked away from the overt display of emotion. It was too much. How could someone hold that much grief and still live? She shuddered, unable and unwilling to imagine losing any of the people she cared about most. Her gaze landed on Mort. His eyes were filled with a deep sadness and her heart throbbed in her chest, as if it was too heavy to carry her love for him.

Cressida nudged her leg, rubbing against her and Fi bent down to stroke her head. Her calf pulsed where the bitemark was branded into her skin. She didn't want to lose her familiar, her friend or Mort. Why was this what it took to realise she was an idiot? She should have told him how she felt, why she was so scared of marriage, of losing herself as a person in the joining of a couple. But instead, she'd risked driving him away completely because she couldn't face her issues and be honest.

"Mort…" she began.

A metallic noise made her turn. Hetty picked up the knife from where it had fallen on the floor and held it up.

"You couldn't let me have him," she wailed.

"It's over, Hetty. It wasn't him."

Fi gave her a pitying look as the woman shook her head, looking less like an evil necromancer and simply like a mother who had lost her child. The knife went limp in her hand. Fi got to her knees and edged towards Hetty, hand outstretched like she was comforting a child.

"It's OK, just give me the knife and this will all be over."

"It is all over." There was a sharpness to the woman's voice and Fi stopped her approach. How did you deal with a grieving mother? Agatha would know, but she wasn't here.

Hetty glanced at the tech witch before she turned back to her son. She stroked his golden hair once, her lip wobbling and tears streaming down her cheeks.

Hetty raised the knife to her own neck, pricking the skin.

"No!" Fi lunged forward. Too slowly.

The necromancer drew the blade over her throat and slumped over her son.

Fi made it to her side. Too late. She turned the woman over and pressed her hands against the cut, hot blood pouring through her fingers.

Hetty mouthed something, her words garbled through the dark liquid as she coughed it up in raking bubbles. Then she was still. Fi pressed against the wound until Mort came to her side and gently lifted her up.

"She's gone, Fi."

Numb, Fi let him lead her outside.

Chapter 42

Detective Ledd met them outside the front door. "What happened–?" He broke off as he clocked the dead bodies and the pool of blood in the hall.

"There's more in the kitchen," Fi managed before she slumped down against the wall. Cressida curled up by her side, lending her comfort through their shared bond. Fi rested one bloodied hand on the wyrm's golden scales.

The detective blustered past them into the house, muttering under his breath about bloody witches. Fi rubbed her leg, then hugged her knees. This was it. This was how it ended. Not, as she'd expected, stuck in a virtual reality headset surrounded by pizza boxes, probably from a heart attack brought on by excessive gaming and a poor lifestyle, but here in this hallway next to two corpses. She swallowed. Best to go quickly, not prolong the agony. She didn't want to be a zombie.

Fi turned to Mort with her eyes filled with tears. "I'm so sorry. I love you, just know that."

He embraced her then pulled away. "Why are you talking like you're about to die?"

She pulled up her jeans and pointed to her calf where two semi-circular teeth marks curved in jagged crescents through her skin, leaking blood. Mort bent over and studied them.

"It's only a matter of time," she said. "Just, kill me now. Make it quick. I don't want to be a zombie."

His mouth pulled up at one corner.

"I'm glad you find my death funny." She buried her face in her hands. Why did she still push him away, even when she was at death's door? "Sorry. Just do it."

He took her hands in his and pulled them away from her face. "Sorry, I shouldn't laugh. But you're not going to turn into a zombie. It wasn't a virus driving them, it was magic. But, we should get it checked out at the hospital, who knows what bacteria they had. You probably need a rabies shot."

Fi stopped her sigh of relief. "That's really comforting, you know that."

He shrugged and gave her a lopsided smile before pulling her to her feet.

Don't ever worry me like that again, Cressida said, sending a small smoke ring up in relief.

Detective Ledd reappeared; his face almost green behind his trimmed moustache. "You couldn't have called for back-up?"

"There wasn't time…" Fi gave up trying to explain, and limped away, gripping Mort's arm for support.

"Where are you going?" the detective asked.

“Hospital. Don’t worry. I’ll write you a report.”

Chapter 43

A dark portal opened up in front of them. Fi jumped back, her eyes boggling. Mort sighed.

"It looks like Arawn wants to see us."

That no good piece of–

"Cressida! OK, well we stopped the necromancer, so maybe he wants to say thank you."

Mort snorted. "In my experience, gods don't say thank you."

"Guess we should go see what he wants."

"Together?" Mort held out his hand and Fi grasped it, interlinking their fingers.

"Together."

Together, echoed Cressida.

Fi bent to scoop up the small wyrm. They stepped through the portal. Fi closed her eyes but it didn't stem the wave of nausea that washed over her. When she opened them again, they were in a field of swaying golden grass, with small star shaped flowers scattered among the tall thin blades of grass.

She stumbled and gripped Mort harder as her leg thrummed with pain. She gritted her teeth against it.

"It's beautiful," Fi said, trying to ignore her throbbing leg.

Mort pulled her close. "Welcome to Annwn, the land of the dead."

"It wasn't like this before."

THE OTHER REALM FORMS TO MY DESIRES. THIS IS WHERE SOULS CAN ENJOY THEIR AFTERLIFE. IN GREEK MYTHOLOGY, IT WAS KNOWN AS THE ELYSIAN FIELDS, IN OTHER TONGUES, IT IS CALLED PARADISE.

Fi whirled around at the voice, expecting the huge skull that had shimmered in the night sky. Instead, a tall, cloaked figure strode across the field, surrounded by lean, white hunting dogs with russet red ears. They flowed through the grass with inhuman speed and lay down in front of the two mortals, not even out of breath.

THESE ARE MY HOUNDS.

Fi held out her hand to the closest one and it nuzzled her palm, its hot breath almost burning her skin. She stroked its soft ear, marvelling at the pure redness of it, like a sunrise or sunset as it glistened in the twilight of the other realm.

YOU ARE HONOURED. THEY DO NOT OFTEN PERMIT THE TOUCH OF MORTALS.

My witch is no ordinary mortal. Cressida bared her teeth at the god.

"Thanks Cress."

NO SHE IS NOT.

And you can stop fawning over those dogs any time you like.

Fi looked up and took a step backwards. The cloaked figure was right in front of them now, having covered the distance of the field in a blink of an eye.

Arawn's skull head was in proportion with his human shaped body, and his ram horns swept back and around, their gold tips shimmering as he turned his head.

CONGRATULATIONS, MORTIMER GREGORIUS DE'ATH AND FIONA JOULES BLAIR.

Mort bowed his head. Fi copied him and muttered, "No problem."

YOU HAVE DONE WELL.

The skull nodded once in acknowledgement.

Fi stayed quiet, her hand linked with Mort's. What was the protocol when a god thanked you? She decided to state facts. "We destroyed the book."

I KNOW. IT WAS ABOUT TIME THAT THE KNOWLEDGE WAS REMOVED FROM MANKIND. IT IS TOO DANGEROUS. Arawn paused. I PROMISED YOU A BOON IF YOU SUCCEEDED.

"Oh, there's no need–" Mort started.

Fi elbowed Mort in the side. "It could be handy to have a god on our side," she hissed.

A GOD NEVER BREAKS THEIR PROMISE. TO YOU, MORTIMER GREGORIUS DE'ATH, FAITHFUL SERVANT, I GRANT THE OPTION OF FREEDOM.

Mort's face turned up, his eyes wide in disbelief. "You mean it?"

The night sky swirled with dark storm clouds and the neon light of Arawn's green eyes narrowed in their skull sockets. DO YOU DOUBT MY WORD?

Mort bowed his head. "Never, my lord."

WHEN YOU ARE READY, YOU MAY LEAVE MY SERVICE.

Mort sank to his knees and held out his sword to the god.

DO NOT BE HASTY, YOUNG MORTIMER. IF YOU LEAVE MY SERVICE, YOU LOSE THE POWERS I GRANT YOU.

"I know what I want. And being at someone else's beck and call isn't it."

VERY WELL. I RESPECT YOUR WISH. WHEN YOU PLACE THE SWORD BACK IN ITS SCABBARD, YOU SHALL NO LONGER BE MY SERVANT. BUT IF YOU EVER WISH TO RETURN TO MY SERVICE AND MY PROTECTION, SIMPLY DRAW THE SWORD AND IT SHALL BE DONE.

Mort bowed his head and returned the sword to the scabbard. It disappeared from its spot at his waist with a flash of neon green light.

"Mort?"

"I'm free," he gazed at Fi with wide eyed wonderment. "My family is free."

The polished skull grinned down at them and Fi wondered if there was a trick somewhere in the God of Death's promise.

AND FIONA JOULES BLAIR, WITCH OF LIGHTNING. TO YOU I GIFT THE …

"Actually, I do have a favour to ask."

Be careful, Cressida hissed in her mind. *You can't trust him.*

The god inclined his skull head.

Fi coughed. "There's these gnomes, they're gnomeless, I mean homeless and I would really like it if you could help with that. Please."

Arawn stared at her, his green eyes seeming to weigh her soul. YOU ASK FOR SOMETHING FOR OTHERS.

"I do." She linked her hand with Mort's. "I have everything I need."

IT SHALL BE DONE.

"Although, if you have the latest console knocking about in that robe…" Mort nudged her in the ribs. "Never mind."

Epilogue

Fi watched as the gnomes lined up and waddled to their new home. She wasn't sure that a burial mound in the middle of the Cotswolds was the most inconspicuous site for the gnome-ads but Arawn had told her the site was protected and they would have access to the spirit realm as well.

The god had visited her at home to tell her that tidbit. Fi had nodded politely and told him it wasn't usual to portal into people's bathrooms. Arawn hadn't seemed to notice her fumbling with a hastily grabbed towel that was too small to adequately cover everything that modern decency required. She shuddered at the memory and was relieved when Priapus brought her back to the present.

"Thank you, kind witch. If you ever have need of anything, we gnomes will repay you." Priapus bowed.

Fi smiled. "Not a problem. All part of the service. Seriously, don't turn up unannounced in my life. I still don't know how you showed up at the house."

"I followed you of course." That explained nothing. "I have pledged myself to your service and I always honour my vows. Now, let us get to our new home." The gnome leader nodded and joined his people as they shuffled out of sight into the safety of the burial mound.

Fi had pulled her own strings and the Magical Liaison Office had declared the mound to be a site of ancient historical significance and a former toxic waste dump so there was no chance of any tourist visiting the site.

"About time. They terrorised my poor chooks," Agatha said.

Fi suppressed a snort. It was about time the demon cockerel got taken down a peg or two.

Agatha glared at her. "I don't know what you're laughing about. My lawn is in ruins and you should see what they've done to the fruit bushes. The topiary nearly gave Mum a heart attack and Harris turned up to take a picture for 'inspiration' for his next most humorous vegetable in show."

This time, Fi released her laugh and wiped a tear from her eye. Her sister's lips twitched too and then she burst out laughing. Mort shook his head as he watched the two sisters sharing their moment of mirth.

Agatha let out a final giggle and inhaled deeply. "Right, I'm off. Got to make sure Bea's all ready for school tomorrow. You don't need the car anymore, do you?"

"No thanks, I'm not taking any of them back with us."

Agatha nodded and left. Fi leaned against Mort and they watched in silence until the last gnome had disappeared from view.

"So, now the necromancer is dealt with, can we talk?"

Fi's heart fluttered against her ribcage. Mort sounded so serious. But she couldn't avoid it any longer. She swallowed. Like her sister said, it wasn't like she wanted anyone else. So she should just woman up and agree to marry him. Her stomach felt like it was tied in knots. Why did commitment scare her so much? He looked her straight in the eyes. She'd taken too long to reply. The least she could do was hear him out. "Sure."

"There's something I've wanted to ask you for a while. I want to take our relationship to the next level."

Levelling up. Like in a videogame. She could do that. That nausea in her stomach was just excitement. Not nerves.

Stop panicking. He's perfect for you, Cressida said.

"But if it's not something you want, you can tell me and that's fine. It won't change how I feel about you."

Why did he have to be so understanding and in touch with his feelings? It was sickening.

"You know I love you, and I want to be with you. I want to commit to you. I have committed to you. And I think you feel the same."

Fi nodded. She didn't trust herself to speak.

"So Fiona Blair," he took a small velvet box from his jacket pocket and held it out to her, "will you–"

"I can't!"

"Oh, right. OK."

"I mean, I love you, but we've only been together properly for a few months, and it's too soon. I can't marry you."

"Marry?" Mort's forehead crinkled.

Fi screwed up her face. "Weren't you going to ask me to marry you?"

He let out a burst of relieved laughter. "No."

"Oh." It wasn't that funny, was it? He had tears in his eyes.

He opened the box to reveal a key. "I wanted to ask if you'd move in with me. We practically live together as it is, so I wanted to make it official."

Fi's heart soared.

"But I understand if–"

She launched herself at him and wrapped her arms around him. "Of course I want to move in with you."

It was Mort's turn to look confused. "You do? Really?"

"Of course."

"But you said–"

Fi pressed a finger to his lips. "Forget what I said. I'm an idiot. I'd love to move in with you, Mortimer Gregorius De'ath." She replaced her finger with her lips and kissed him hard.

Thank you

A special thank you to my amazing patrons: Emma Ward and Mark Canty who always support me.

If you want to support Gemma, you can find her on www.patreon.com/G_Clatworthy for exclusive first reads of new stories.

You can also join her newsletter at www.gemmaclatworthy.com for short story about one of the witches in the Omensford series and follow Gemma on www.instagram.com/gemmaclatworthy, www.facebook.com/gemmaclatworthy or join the Facebook reader's group Gemma's book wyrms.

You can also join her newsletter for a free prequel to her Rise of Dragons series and follow Gemma at www.instagram.com/gemmaclatworthy, www.facebook.com/gemmaclatworthy or join the reader's group Gemma's book wyrms.

About the Author

Gemma started writing during the 2020 lockdown and loves fantasy fiction and dragons in particular. She lives in Wiltshire with her family and two cats and also enjoys crafts of all kinds. You can see all her writing on patreon. Join the conversation at Gemma's book wyrms readers' group on Facebook.

She also writes children's books. You can find out more on her website www.gemmaclatworthy.com or follow her on Instagram (www.instagram.com/gemmaclatworthy) or Facebook (www.facebook.com/gemmaclatworthy).

Other Books by G Clatworthy

Books in the Rise of the Dragons series:

Awakening

Solstice of Dragons

Equinox Betrayal

Darkest Deception

Attack on Avalon

Fated Bloodlines

Eat, Pray, Dragons

Books in the Omensford series (set in the Rise of the Dragons universe):

Bedsocks and Broomsticks

Cream Teas and Crystal Balls

Donkeys and Demons

Pumpkins and Popstars

Exes and Enchantments

Fae and Familiars

Gnomes and Necromancy

Books in the Saffron Vale series (a cozy fantasy series, part of the Cozy Vales universe):

A Colour to Dye For

Going for Guild

Commission Impossible